8/19

osbkm

THE LAST CONFESSION OF RICK O'SHEA

Irishman Rick O'Shea decides the time has come to give up his life of banditry and return to his own country — but his plans are thrown into disarray when, at the urging of a priest, he delays his voyage in order to undertake the rescue of a child being held to ransom across the border in Mexico. Caught between a vicious band of cutthroats on one side and a crooked lawman on the other, O'Shea's chances of getting back to Ireland in one piece seem to dwindle by the minute . . .

Books by Clyde Barker
in the Linford Western Library:

LONG SHADOWS

CLYDE BARKER

THE LAST CONFESSION OF RICK O'SHEA

Complete and Unabridged

LINFORD
Leicester

First published in Great Britain in 2017 by
Robert Hale
an imprint of The Crowood Press
Wiltshire

First Linford Edition
published 2019
by arrangement with
The Crowood Press
Wiltshire

A catalogue record for this book is available
from the British Library.

ISBN 978–1–4448–4206–7

Published by
F. A. Thorpe (Publishing)
Anstey, Leicestershire

Set by Words & Graphics Ltd.
Anstey, Leicestershire
Printed and bound in Great Britain by
T. J. International Ltd., Padstow, Cornwall

This book is printed on acid-free paper

1

The bar-room of the Girl of the Period saloon was all but deserted; the time still lacking twenty minutes until noon and the midday rush consequently not yet having begun. Apart from a small group seated at a table the only patrons were two men leaning against the counter while supping glasses of porter. One was a mean, ferrety-looking man of perhaps five-and-twenty years of age, the other looked to be five or ten years older. The two of them were chatting in a desultory fashion.

'So it's really true?' asked the younger of the two men. 'You're goin' to dig up and sail back across the water to your own country?'

'That I am,' replied the other in a broad Irish brogue. 'I've had about enough o' this benighted country and its ways. I've a mind to see my family again, settle down and take up farming.'

'I reckon as you'll miss the life here,' observed his companion shrewdly. 'You won't find switching from road agent to sodbuster so easy as you might think.'

'Will ye hush your damned mouth now? We needn't share my business with all the world and his dog.'

At that point an acquaintance of the younger man entered the saloon. After making his excuses to the Irishman with whom he was currently drinking, the fellow who had caused his vexation went off to speak with his friend, leaving Rick O'Shea to his own thoughts. He glanced uneasily up to the clock, which hung on the wall above the bar. It showed that there were now just seventeen minutes to noon and the unwelcome confrontation which he was due to face at that hour. To distract himself O'Shea began to leaf through a copy of the *Pecos County Advertiser Incorporating the San Angelo Agricultural Gazette and Intelligencer*, which somebody had left on the bar. It was dated September 3 1879, showing that it was less than a week old. O'Shea's eye fell upon a headline that announced: LOCAL CHILD SEIZED BY BANDITS. As he read the article that followed, Rick O'Shea shook his head disapprovingly. This was the kind of crime that he detested.

Citizens in our own fair corner of this state will no doubt be shocked and dismayed to learn of the unparalleled outrage which took place near San Angelo on the 1st Inst. Local rancher THOMAS COVENAY rose in the morning of that day, only to find that his youngest daughter EMILY was missing from her bedroom. The little girl, who is but 12 years of age, had, as far as can be apprehended, been snatched from her home in order to extract a ransom from MR COVENAY. A note on the child's bed demanded the sum of $10,000 for the safe release of EMILY. We are reliably informed that such is the state of business at MR COVENAY's spread, that he would be exceedingly fortunate to be able to summon up a tenth of this amount.

Your reporter spoke to Sheriff SETH JACKSON, who, while expressing his determination to hunt down the villains responsible for this dreadful crime, intimated that it is supposed among himself and his assistants that the girl has been spirited away across the Rio Grande to Mexico; out of reach of the forces of law and order. In the meantime, the lately widowed MR COVENAY and his other daughter, JEMIMA, are distraught with anxiety and fear.

After finishing the short piece O'Shea tutted to himself. Although he too was a robber — some would even say bandit — there were depths to which he would never sink. Harming children was, according to his lights, as low as one could get.

The minute-hand on the clock above the bar jerked forward. It was now a quarter to twelve and Richard Finnegan O'Shea knew that, little as he might wish to do so, he would soon be forced to face, unwillingly, a man whom he had no desire to meet and from whom he had, in a sense, been fleeing for the better part of fifteen years. He downed the last contents of his glass and stood up. He might just as well get it over with. For the first time since he had left his home and country in the winter of 1868, Rick O'Shea was about to make his confession in the Catholic church, which stood across the square from the saloon.

O'Shea knew full well that if he arrived back in County Donegal and let slip to his mother that he hadn't so much as set foot in church since taking ship for America, then she would never recover from the shock of it. He had been raised in the most staunchly Catholic family one could imagine; his mother was a regular communicant not only on Sundays, but on various weekday mornings as well. For his own part, young Richard had never really taken to religion, but would not have dared to oppose his mother in the matter. No sooner had he left home, however, than he dropped churchgoing entirely.

Now, with the prospect of seeing his mother in a matter of months, he was aware that one of the first questions she would ask him on his return would be: 'And when did you last make your confession?' This, to his mother, was the infallible touchstone of virtue. No matter how a man lived his life, if he only went to confession each week he was on the right path.

It would have sat ill with O'Shea to greet his mother after such a long absence and immediately tell her a falsehood when, as she certainly would, she asked when last he had been to confession. The obvious solution would be for him to be in a position where he was able to state truthfully that he had seen to the welfare of his immortal soul just a few days before leaving the United States. With luck his mother would not pursue the matter and ask how long ago had been the time before that!

The interior of the church was cool and dark. It smelled of beeswax polish and incense; scents, to Rick O'Shea, that were redolent of sanctity. He was at once transported back to his childhood, spending every Sunday in a church that smelled precisely the same as this one. O'Shea saw, to his irritation that, despite arriving a minute or two before the designated hour for the hearing of confession, he was not the first in line. A desiccated and shrivelled-up little woman, swathed in black, was already sitting by the booth, waiting for the priest to enter from the other side. *What the devil can she have to confess?* he thought wrathfully. He had just wished to get the business out of the way, yet now he would be obliged to sit here, cooling his heels, while this wretched little woman regaled the priest with a long list of trifling misdemeanours and imaginary sins. There it was, though: there was nothing to be done. O'Shea settled himself down on the bench and thought about how good it would be to see his own country again after all these years.

Very few men managed to thrive for long as outlaws in those days. Sure, they occasionally made fabulous sums of money but, as fast as cash was acquired it was frittered away on liquor and women. It was a rare individual who existed on the wrong side of the law and managed to save any of his ill-gotten gains, storing them away against future need. Besides which, the career of the average outlaw was generally measured in months rather than years. Those who didn't get themselves killed in gunfights, either with the law or after falling out with former comrades, generally ending up being hanged, legally or otherwise, or, failing that, incarcerated in the state penitentiary for years.

Rick O'Shea was different. His banditry was calculated and restrained. He had come to the United States to improve his lot and that of his family back home. His aim had been plain and simple: to make enough money to send back to his family to ensure that they were freed for ever from the grinding poverty in which he had been raised. In particular he hoped to see his beloved mother settled in a little freehold property of her own, freed from the constant threat of eviction by an absentee English landlord. He had succeeded in this endeavour and now hoped to reap for himself the benefits of his industry.

By being systematic and cautious in his depredations, never too greedy or taking too many risks, and also by moving regularly across the country, O'Shea had managed to live modestly but quite comfortably while also sending regular sums of money back to his family. This had enabled his brother to buy a small farm and expand it over the years. Richard O'Shea had come to America as a boy of nineteen and now, at the age of thirty, he was looking forward to returning to his own country and living the life of a well-to-do farmer and all that went with such a station in life.

Yes, he reflected as he sat waiting to enter the confessional booth, he hadn't done at all badly. He had even budgeted for whatever penance he might incur for the sins he was about to confess. Obviously, after eleven years of theft, coupled with the occasional murder, he could hardly expect to be given a couple of Hail Marys to recite. But that was fine; a sum of $1,000 had been set aside for the missionary fund or whatever else the church needed. O'Shea had it all planned out to a nicety.

At last the old woman shuffled out.

O'Shea stood up and entered the dark booth, which was little larger than a broom closet. The priest was a shadowy silhouette on the other side of the grille. O'Shea knelt down and muttered the ritual words:

'Bless me Father, for I have sinned.'

On hearing the traditional response, Rick O'Shea's heart sank. In as strong an accent as his own, one which sounded to O'Shea suspiciously like a Donegal brogue, the priest asked:

'And how long is it, my son, since your last confession?' An Irish priest! This was the last thing O'Shea wanted. Being so close to the border, he had half-hoped that he might find a Mexican in charge here; some simpleton who would not ask too many searching questions and likely to be vastly impressed with an offering of $1,000. Dealing with an Irishman — and from his own county at that — was a horse of a different colour.

By the time he had admitted to innumerable robberies, the odd killing, various woundings and a several adulterous liaisons, O'Shea mentally raised the amount that he might have to pay as a penance. When he had finished reciting the sorry catalogue there was a silence for a moment; he wondered if the priest was too shocked to be able come up with any response. When the man did at last speak, he said:

'Are ye a good shot, my son?'

This was so unexpected that O'Shea couldn't quite credit the evidence of his ears and had to ask for the question to be repeated, which the priest did impatiently.

'It's a simple enough question,' he said. 'Would you say that you're a good shot?'

'Better than most, I guess.'

'I'm not asking you to guess!' burst out the priest with the greatest irascibility. 'Recollect where you are and answer the question truthfully.'

'Then I'm the best shot you're ever like to meet.'

'And from all I am able to make out

from what I've just heard, you've no scruple about killing; is that right?'

Where all this was leading Rick O'Shea had not the remotest idea. He had never in all his life heard a man of God speak in this way.

'I wouldn't say I have no scruple about killing, Father,' he answered slowly. 'I've killed men, to be sure, but only in self-defence. When they were after killing me, you understand.'

'You're a thief, an adulterer and murderer is what it amounts to. Nothing worse — that you've held back?'

'Isn't that bad enough?' asked O'Shea, still not sure where things were heading. 'I come here seeking absolution. I thought that I could make some slight recompense by helping you establish a school or something. Paying for a mission station, maybe . . .'

Through the grille that separated them came a short, barking laugh.

'So you thought you'd buy your way

to salvation, is that how it is? You won't get off so cheap, don't think it for a moment. You ever hear of a fellow called Yanez?'

'Valentin Yanez? Sure. He's a rare villain. Mexican, though he operates over on this side o' the border odd times. Why?'

For a few seconds the priest was silent. Then he said:

'Yanez and his men have stolen away the child of one of my parishioners. She's but a little girl and her father is distracted with the horror of it all.'

'That the ransom case? I read about it. Can't he just pay up?'

'The family are poor as church mice. Land rich, but cash poor. Yanez won't take a cent less than ten thousand dollars. I've heard it said that he'd not hesitate to kill the child if he doesn't get the money — as an encouragement to his next victim, if you take my meaning. To show that he's not a man to be trifled with.'

'It's a filthy business, but I don't see

what it has to do with me.'

'Do ye not? Then you've duller wits than I gave ye credit for. I mean for you to fetch little Emily Covenay back to her family. That's all.'

It was not often that Rick O'Shea was altogether lost for words, but this was certainly one of those times. He felt as though somebody had just knocked him down. Haltingly, he tried to express his feelings.

'But that's a job for the law,' he said. 'I wouldn't know where to start. You can't mean that you're hoping to use me like a mercenary or aught of the sort? This is a blazing strange conversation!'

'I've been praying as hard as I know how for little Emily Covenay, asking the good Lord to send me help. Looks like you're all that's on offer. It can't be helped. You're not the one I'd have chosen, left to me own devices, but there it is.

'Now listen, until you undertake this penance your very soul is at stake. You hear what I tell you? You're in a state of mortal sin and if you die in any way other than in pursuit of this task, then the Devil will be waiting at your side to drag you off to hell. You understand that? It's your only hope for forgiveness for the dreadful life you've been leading.'

'You mean I'll not be shriven until I do this thing?'

'You got it, my boy. Off you go now — what are ye waiting for? You've a job to do. *Ego te absolvo:* your sins are forgiven you, as long as you carry on with this matter until the child is back with her family. Off with you now.'

As O'Shea got to his feet the priest fired one last parting salvo, saying:

'Whist! Don't think that you're to profit from this in any way. If there's any reward, bounty, what have you, for doing this thing, you're to bring it straight here and hand it over to the church, you hear me? Go on now, you've got a job of work to do.'

Rick O'Shea left the church looking

like a man who has been playing cards for ruinously high stakes and has lost everything in the process. He had entered the place in full expectation of catching the railroad train the next day, then taking ship for Ireland as soon as he'd fetched up in New York. Now, he hardly knew what he was to do. He knew that he could not go back and meet his mother while in a state of mortal sin; it would be the death of her.

There was also his own fear to contend with. The old priest's warning that the Devil would carry him off if he died other than on the track of Yanez and his captive had struck a terrible chill into O'Shea's heart. There had been times, it was true, when Rick O'Shea had doubted the very existence of God, but of the Devil, never. He had seen abundant evidence of the Devil's work too often to think him a bogyman dreamed up to frighten children.

There was nothing for it but to do as he had been bid and try to restore this child to her family. It was damned nuisance, but there it was. For all that he saw himself as a man free from superstition and with no fear of any man, O'Shea's early raising had left an indelible mark upon his character. He might, indeed did, break all the commandments, but he knew that there *were* commandments and that there was usually a reckoning in the long run for disregarding them.

Never once did it cross his mind simply to ignore what the old priest had said and carry on as he had been planning to do for some months. His only hope of starting a new life back in old Ireland and being at peace was to undertake this wretched commission that had been laid upon him. Why, if he just cut and ran now, he wouldn't even be able to attend church with his mammy when he got home to Donegal.

The first step would be to see if anybody knew where Yanez and his gang were presently situated. O'Shea recalled that the young fellow to whom he had earlier been talking in the saloon was said to smuggle goods across the Rio Grande to evade duty. A good first move might be to consult with him.

★   ★   ★

The Girl of the Period was much more lively than it had been when O'Shea had gone off to make his confession. They generally did good business between midday and about two or three o'clock. Jack Flynn, the fellow he wished to speak to, was standing in the middle of a group of his cronies. He and O'Shea had undertaken one job together a matter of six months previously. It had paid well enough, but by God, Flynn was a mad one! Several people had died needlessly in the raid that they had launched and he had sworn never again to work with the younger man.

O'Shea went over to Flynn and asked if he would favour him with a few words, away from the others. There was little privacy to be found in the crowded saloon, so O'Shea simply lowered his voice and said:

'Tell me now, you know where that Mexican fellow Yanez is to be found?'

'Yanez? Man alive! You're not wanting to be gettin' yourself mixed up with that one. Why are you askin'?'

'That don't signify. You know where he is?'

'Well, I guess it's your funeral. Hey, not an hour since you were telling me as you were bound for over the sea and far away. You change your plans or something?'

'Anybody ever tell you that you're a wordy bastard, Flynn?'

Jack Flynn laughed good-naturedly.

'Now you mention it, the suggestion has been made once or twice. Seriously, I'd keep clear of Yanez. Listen. Me and a few others have somethin' in mind, away over, up by the Reds. You want in?'

'Will you just hush up and tell me where he's to be found? It's important.'

'Sure. He operates out of a spot just

over the river. Village called Cuchu-verachi. Yanez has got family over that way. He's built himself a walled compound near the village, place like a little fort. He crosses over, raids somewhere and then hops back over the Rio Grande, where he can't be touched. Even the Mexican army steers clear of some bits of the border over that way. Stand on this bank, nigh to the ferry, an' you can just make out Chuchuverachi, away over on the other side.'

O'Shea rubbed his chin thoughtfully.

'That all sounds as I thought it might be,' he said. 'How many men does Yanez's band of cut-throats run to, would you say?'

Flynn shrugged. 'Couldn't rightly say. Varies somewhat. Seven or eight, maybe?'

'Thanks,' said O'Shea; then, as he turned to go, 'You been a great help.' Moving off, he brushed against a table, knocking something off it. He looked down to see a clay pipe fall to the sawdust-strewn floor, where it shattered.

'Hey, you clumsy son of a bitch!' somebody growled. 'You done broke my best pipe.'

At that time it was not uncommon for those seeking to make a little money for drink to balance an old clay pipe, worth a dime at most, near the back of some likely-looking stranger standing in a bar. Sooner or later he would move and knock it to the ground, whereupon the aggrieved owner would sweep the shattered fragments from the floor, thrust them into his pocket and claim that it had been his favourite meerschaum or something of the sort.

Rick O'Shea turned to the fellow with a savage and unholy joy bubbling up within his breast. He had been feeling mightily ticked off at having that padre railroad him into this enterprise, but he could hardly beat up on a priest. This man, though, was simply begging to be taught a lesson. O'Shea had just twisted round to confront him when he realized with a sickening dread that it would not do at all. Suppose the man pulled a gun on him — or even just a knife? He recollected vividly what he had been told: that if he died other than in the course of rescuing the child, then he was damned for all eternity.

One or two of the men standing near by watched the developing scene with interest and pleasurable anticipation. Rick O'Shea was known to some of those there as a man who would take no nonsense from anybody and was well able to handle himself in a rough-house. They were destined to be disappointed. O'Shea was not about to jeopardize his immortal soul for the sake of some trifling quarrel that could be satisfied by the expenditure of a small sum of money. The bully who was baiting O'Shea sensed the fire going out of him and exulted in the realization that he was about to skin another rube for the price of a few drinks.

'That pipe cost me five dollars,' he said.

Without saying a word O'Shea took out a ten-dollar piece and spun it towards the man with his thumb. The gratified and surprised look on the wretch's face was comical. Less amusing were the contemptuous looks on the faces of some of the spectators to this little comedy; men who plainly thought that Rick O'Shea must be going soft. He gritted his teeth, turned on his heel and left the Girl of the Period to go back to the hotel where he had been staying. The sooner he embarked upon this fool's errand and got it out of the way, the better.

2

It was a glorious day to be out in the wild country. The land was parched and faded after the long, hot summer, but it was still a joy to be riding along with the sun on his face and the wind behind him. The intense irritation that Rick O'Shea had felt towards the priest yesterday had abated somewhat and given way to a reluctant admiration at the sheer nerve of the man. He really must have seen O'Shea's turning up that day as the answer to his prayers and, you had to hand it to him, he had taken full advantage of the situation. Seldom had a hand been better played.

There was another factor which caused O'Shea not to feel overly downhearted at the turn of events, which was that the account in the newspaper of the little girl's plight had actually touched his heart and aroused his pity. Somebody ought to do something about such a vile deed as snatching a child from her family. Since the law didn't seem minded to act, well, then there was some sense in an individual such as he tackling the problem. He was certainly better equipped to do so than the average fellow.

Yes, if anybody could undertake such a ticklish job as this, then Rick O'Shea was the boy to do it. So it was that, as he rode along, O'Shea began to hum a merry tune. With a little good fortune he would be able to deal with this affair in a week or so and still be on board a ship in New York within a fortnight. After all his thieving it was a novel experience to be riding on the side of right for a change.

★　★　★

Shimmering on the horizon ahead of O'Shea was the mighty chain of rugged peaks known as the 'Reds', on account

26

of their colour. This range of mountains, rising in places to 5,000 feet or more, stretched for over a hundred and fifty miles, blocking off that part of the Rio Grande for which he was heading. Fortunately there was a pass, just one, which cut right through the middle of the mountains and would bring him out twenty miles or so from the town for which he was aiming.

At some time in the distant past the earth had shifted slightly and opened up a gap between two towering crags. This had created a miniature valley which had been used over the years as a way to reach the river. When the railroad arrived the pass had been greatly widened with the help of explosives, until now both a railroad line and a passable road ran through the gap in the Reds. Another couple of hours should bring him into view of what was universally known as Grey John's Gap. Why it bore this sobriquet nobody seemed to know.

It was an hour or two past noon

when Rick O'Shea eventually approached Grey John's Gap and realized that things might be about to turn a little complicated. A mile or so from the beginning of the pass he could see a group of men milling around by the railroad line. As he drew nearer O'Shea's heart sank. He had lived by dishonesty for so many years that he had a sixth sense when he encountered men about to steal something or harm others. The furtive-looking manoeuvres around the railroad line at which he was currently looking bore all the hallmarks of a half-dozen men up to no good. So it proved, for when he rode on to the pass the first man he saw turned out to be Jack Flynn. Flynn greeted him amiably enough.

'O'Shea!' he cried. 'Hope you ain't minded to muscle in on this little enterprise of ours. I offered you in yesterday, if you recall, and you turned me down flat.'

'I don't want any part of this,' said

O'Shea, hastily. He was aware that Flynn's companions were eyeing him with disfavour, like he was going to cheat them out of something. 'What are you boys about here, anyways?'

'It's all right,' called Jack Flynn to the men who had stopped what they were doing in order to stare suspiciously at O'Shea, 'he's one of us.' He addressed himself directly to O'Shea again:

'What it is, man, is this. You know the line here turns west once it passes through the gap? There's a spur as goes on to the goldfield at Jackson's Landing. Train brings the stuff through here once a week. We's goin' to stop it and kind o' take all the gold they's got.'

'It's not to be thought of!' exclaimed O'Shea without thinking. 'You'll have the whole area crawling with lawmen in next to no time.'

'Who're you to say what's not to be thought of?' growled one of the men standing near by. 'You ain't the law, I s'pose?'

'Not a bit of it, but I have important business. I don't want you fellows queering my pitch. You rob that train and I head south from here, folk're apt to think as I had a hand in it.'

'We don't got time for this,' said another of the men. 'Time's pressing. You move on, mister. It's nothing to do with you.'

This was just the sort of foolishness that O'Shea could do without right now. He could see clearly how, with a little bit of ill fortune, he would wind up under suspicion for a crime with which he had no connection at all. There had been several robberies of this sort lately in and around Pecos County; a posse would be sworn in at once if anything similar were to happen here. It would be just his luck to be caught up in this; particularly where he had been seen by everybody talking with Jack Flynn in the Girl of the Period not forty-eight hours previously. Playing for time, he asked casually:

30

'How you going to stop this train?'

Flynn laughed. 'Why, we's goin' to dynamite the tracks. Lookee here.' He went over to one of his companions and came back with three cartridges of dynamite, which were lashed together with wire. 'Going for to blow up the track, so's the driver sees it. He'll stop and then we move in. Nobody need get hurt if they do as they're told.'

'When's it due?' asked O'Shea, wondering if he had time to ride hard and be clear of the place before the lightning fell. A second later there came a shout from a ledge up above them which presumably gave a good vantage point for a view of the way ahead.

'She's a-comin',' hollered the man. 'Best get that fuse lit.'

At which point Rick O'Shea found himself being wholly disregarded by Jack Flynn and the others. Flynn ran to the railroad tracks and bent down, placing his deadly package against one of the rails. O'Shea heard the mournful note of the locomotive's whistle in the distance. He watched helplessly as Flynn struck a lucifer, ignited the fuse, then jumped up and began sprinting for the cover of some nearby boulders where the rest of the party had already taken shelter.

'You better run for it, man,' Flynn shouted.

Spurring on the mare, O'Shea cantered towards the rocks where the others were sheltering; he got there just as the dynamite went off like a clap of thunder. Looking back, he saw a column of dust and smoke rising from the tracks. At that same moment the railroad train hove into view. Seeing the aftermath of the explosion, and most likely having heard it as well, the driver applied the brakes with a screeching of steel on steel. The mighty locomotive ground slowly to a halt.

As it did so Rick O'Shea reflected grimly that this was just precisely why he had only ridden with Flynn the once. The fellow's jobs were always chaotic and disorganized. How he had so far avoided being killed or imprisoned was something of a mystery to O'Shea.

Up until this point O'Shea had figured that he might somehow be able to slip away unremarked by anybody on the train, then just ride on to the Rio Grande to embark upon his quest. His past experience of working with Flynn, though, suggested that this was unlikely and that whatever resulted from this latest, hare-brained exploit of his would throw O'Shea's own plans into disarray.

So it proved. Once the train had come to a halt and Flynn and his fellow robbers had mounted up with a view to riding down on the train and robbing it, a most unexpected thing occurred. A ramp crashed down from a freight wagon at the rear of the train and a party of riders trotted sedately down it as though they had all the time in the world and were about to go for a pleasant ride in the countryside.

Rick O'Shea had not survived as an outlaw for so many years without having developed an uncanny, almost supernatural, ability to spot trouble when it was still a quarter-mile off. This instance was no exception, for the last horse and rider had not left that freight truck before O'Shea had worked out precisely what was about to happen.

There had been three attacks on trains within a radius of perhaps fifty or sixty miles in the last few months. Judging by the casual way that Jack Flynn had been juggling that dynamite around, it was probably a fair guess that he had been at the back of them all. Knowing Flynn, having succeeded once at that game he was likely to carry on until either he blew himself up or was caught and then either jailed or hanged.

It was scarcely surprising that the local law would have been getting tired of this and would now be determined to put a stop to it. No doubt a bunch of temporary deputies had been sworn in and a few decoy trains laid on to see if the bandits might be flushed out. It also struck O'Shea that rumours of some huge shipment of gold would perhaps have been circulated as well, to lure these fools into the trap.

All this flashed through Rick O'Shea's mind in no more than the few seconds it took the riders to leave the train and assemble by the side of the tracks. Almost at the same time, he realized that flight was his only hope here. His being seen sitting on his horse near Flynn and his boys would lead anybody to jump at once to the wholly erroneous conclusion that he himself was a part of this set-up.

As he reached this point in his reasoning the party of horsemen turned their mounts and began trotting towards O'Shea and the others in a leisurely fashion. As they did so they spread out slightly and O'Shea was able to see that there were eight of them in total. There was no other choice for him than to run for it, but perhaps it would be best to wait first for some diversion. If he cut and ran at this moment he could be sure that all eyes would be upon him and at least one of those men would most likely be after him like a shot.

The diversion for which O'Shea was hoping came in the most unforeseen manner; although, knowing Jack Flynn as he did, perhaps he should not have been taken aback by any mad action taken by that individual. Crazy as he was, Flynn's wits were probably as sharp as the next man's when it came to the immediate matter of self-preservation. While O'Shea had been mulling over his possible course of action, Flynn had been taking steps to deal with the sudden reversal that he had encountered. Going by what happened next, he must have had another stick or two of dynamite about his person and have unobtrusively struck a light. All that O'Shea saw was a brief glimpse from the corner of his eye of something flying through the air in the general direction of the other riders; who were still 200 yards away. Then there was a terrific crash, followed by a cloud of dust and smoke which obscured the posse from view. Small stones began falling like hail around O'Shea.

As the echo died down, Jack Flynn gave an unearthly, banshee-like battle cry and, against all reason, led his men in a charge straight at the lawmen. O'Shea could hardly believe his luck. He rode at once to the other side of the tracks and began cantering alongside them towards the train. It was his intention to ride past what promised to be a bloody confrontation in the hope that everybody would be too engrossed in their own affairs to pay him any heed. The gap was closing between the two bodies of armed men to his right and, as long as the riders from the train didn't choose to see him as some kind of flanker who was going to ride fast round behind them and attack from the rear, everything should go just fine.

The plan went like clockwork with just one slight hitch, although it didn't really seem at the time as though it much signified. The snag was that one of the men in the posse knew, and was known to, O'Shea. Presumably Sheriff Seth Jackson was in overall command of the operation to catch the train bandits. He and O'Shea had clashed in the past, although nothing serious had come of their crossing swords with each other.

Now, as O'Shea glanced to his right, there was Seth Jackson, riding on towards the men who had blown up the railroad track. They were separated by a distance of no more than fifty yards. Just at that moment Jackson turned his head and gazed into O'Shea's eyes. Then there came sounds of a few pistol shots. The sheriff's attention was drawn back to the task in which he was presently engaged, but Rick O'Shea knew then that his presence at the scene of this particular crime had been noted. He could only hope that the mischance would not come back to haunt him.

He spurred on his horse and was

soon galloping hell for leather through Grey John's Gap towards the little town of Archangel, which lay on the north bank of the Rio Grande, just across the border from Mexico.

★ ★ ★

Archangel was a dead and alive little burg, with nothing much to recommend it other than the fact that a cable-drawn ferry linked it with Mexico. Inevitably a good deal of smuggling took place across the border at this point. Liquor, tobacco, gold, guns and even women were trafficked to and fro; the movement of goods taking place both from south to north and vice versa.

The authorities on both sides of the border regarded Archangel as a pest-hole but, short of stationing a regiment of infantry permanently on both banks of the Rio Grande at that point, there was little enough to be done about it. Every so often matters got out of hand

and it would be found that, say, Gatling guns rather than just a few rifles were being taken across on the ferry to arm Mexican rebels in the northern provinces. At that point there might be an attempt to crack down for a week or even a month, but sooner or later the forces of law and order would retreat and business would resume.

The ride to Archangel had been uneventful. O'Shea had reined in now and was staring across the broad river from where, almost out of sight on the horizon, could be glimpsed the white-painted houses of what he took to be the village of Chuchuverachi. According to Jack Flynn, the stolen child might well be secreted in or near this village. O'Shea gazed from the landing stage and wondered just how hard this row would be to hoe. Surely Yanez would not be expecting anything so reckless as a raid upon his home territory? The very daring of the thing might take him by surprise and, before the abductor knew what had happened, Rick O'Shea would be back here with the rescued child.

He wasn't one to underestimate the hazards of such a venture: far from it. On the other hand he had been party to some pretty desperate endeavours in the past, which had come off against all the apparent odds. It said something about O'Shea's character that having accepted that he had to do this thing he never once looked back or considered giving up on it. He was a man who, if once he said he would do a thing, would do it, no matter what chanced. That he had unwillingly taken on this little job imposed upon him mattered not a jot.

Restoring that poor little girl to her family was the right and proper thing to do and now that he had been roped into it he knew that he wouldn't rest easy at the thought of the child having her throat cut by some villain who was simply aiming to make a point about his ruthlessness to any future victim.

It was coming on to evening and

there was no percentage in setting out across the border now without having looked around a bit and examined the lie of the land. O'Shea decided therefore to book into one of the little town's two hotels. Although the permanent population of Archangel numbered only 500 souls there was a constantly changing and wildly fluctuating group of transients who needed beds in which to lie. The two so-called 'commercial' hotels catered for these drifters and entrepreneurs.

After booking his room and making provision for the mare in a livery stable on the edge of town, O'Shea thought it might be interesting to hang out in the bar which occupied the ground floor of the hotel at which he was staying. He could see at once that most of the types drinking there were as rough as all get-out. He'd never been to Archangel before and nobody there knew him, at least as far as he was aware.

It would not therefore do to start asking too many probing questions of the clientele, such as *When did you last see Valentin Yanez, the famous bandit leader?* Such a course of action might lead to his being identified as a spy or paid informer, which might in turn end in his being knifed in a darkened alleyway. Better by far to listen to the conversation and see what might be picked up.

Two hours spent in the bar-room yielded absolutely nothing that was germane to O'Shea's purpose. He overheard guarded discussions about shifting 'the gear' in two days and other conversations about men he'd never heard of who would be 'heading south' the next day, but not, as far as he was able to apprehend, any reference, even indirect, to Yanez. He hadn't really thought it likely that he would pick up casual gossip about such an important figure, but it had been worth a try. O'Shea decided to turn in for the night.

Rick O'Shea had always counted it a great blessing that he was possessed of the ability to sink into unconsciousness almost as soon as he laid his head upon the pillow. Come to that, it was the same out on the range, or even lying on a floor somewhere. In the present instance he kicked off his boots, removed his pants and was sound asleep within minutes. He was accordingly slumbering like a baby when he was suddenly catapulted into wakefulness by the unmistakable sound of a pistol being cocked near his ear.

Just as he had a knack or gift for falling easily asleep, so too was Rick O'Shea able to wake instantly with all his senses alert and ready for action. Although the room was in darkness he knew without the shadow of a doubt that somebody was holding a gun to his head. That sharp metallic click as the hammer was pulled back and cocked was one clue, but the clinching proof was the smell of oil from a well-maintained weapon. Impossible to mistake that particular scent for anything else in the world. Without moving a muscle, he said quietly:

'Who are you and what do you want of me?'

'That's the sensible dodge,' said a gruff voice, approvingly. 'I'll light the lamp now, but I can do that with one hand. My pistol's still pointing at you and if you so much as twitch and I'll blow your damned head clean off your shoulders.'

O'Shea was quite prepared to take the man's word for this. He lay still to see how matters might develop. He had no idea why anybody in this town would have taken against him and he was hoping that this was not somebody from his past with an ancient score to settle. The fact that he had been woken up and had not simply had his throat cut while he was sleeping was at least encouraging.

There came the sputtering and flaring of a match and then the soft glow of lamplight spread through the room. Without otherwise moving, O'Shea turned his eyes to see who was menacing him. He beheld a grizzled-looking man well past the first vigour of youth. He had a bristling, iron-grey mustache and two of the coldest and most determined eyes that one could hope to find in a human visage.

'Sheriff Jackson,' said O'Shea amiably, 'this is an unexpected pleasure, to be sure. Had I known you were planning to drop by I would have laid in some comestibles — cakes and ale perhaps, so we could chat over old times.'

'Shut up, O'Shea. You needn't think your blarney is going to do you any good and that's a fact. You'll hang for your work up at the Gap.'

'I'll allow I was up that way, but do you think it would have been such a shambles if I'd been a part of the operation?'

Sheriff Jackson was seated comfortably in the only chair in the room, a rickety wooden structure that had probably started life in somebody's kitchen.

'Like I told you,' he said, 'you ain't

46

going to talk your way out of this. You been dancing 'tween the raindrops for a long, long while and this here's where you get caught in the storm.'

'Mind if I sit up? I can't talk easily sprawled down like this.' Without waiting for an answer O'Shea wriggled about until he was clear of the bedclothes and sitting upright.

'Just bring your hands out from under those covers, real slow, and let me see them,' Jackson said.

O'Shea did so.

'I know you and me got crosswise to each other in the past, Sheriff, but you can't mean to pin that train robbery on me. What happened after I left?'

'After you ran out on your partners, you mean? It was a massacre, that's what happened. Four of your friends were killed and three of my men. That mad fool Flynn lobbed a stick of dynamite, which killed one of his own men and then I shot him. After a bit more fighting they threw down and I sent the two survivors back to San

Angelo in charge of my deputies. Then I came down here to pick you up as well.'

'Is that why you want me? To boost your number of prisoners?' enquired O'Shea innocently. 'I can see where losing a bunch of your men like that would look lousy when you're coming up for re-election soon. But you're backing the wrong pony this time. I was just passing through the Gap on business of my own.'

'Never mind my election. That's my affair. You think I'm going to believe that you just happened to be there when that train was ambushed? I don't think so.'

Rick O'Shea's mind was racing furiously, partly to avoid being sent to jail or even hanged for a crime in which he had had no part, but also because he saw the germ of an idea that might aid him in his own quest.

'I reckon you and me can do business together, Sheriff Jackson,' he said. 'I might be able to do you a good turn.'

Jackson snorted. 'If you think you can

bribe me, then you don't know me at all, that's all I can say on that subject.'

'Lord, but you are a suspicious one. Bribery? Nothing o' the sort. I was thinking maybe of a way to put you in good odour with the citizens of Pecos County and guarantee you get voted in again next month.'

It was obvious from the look on Jackson's face that this was the right tack to take. O'Shea had heard how the good people of San Angelo and the surrounding areas were getting mighty sick of the crimes that were plaguing them. After the train robberies it wasn't hard to guess that the grabbing of a little girl would prove the last straw. You could see where Pecos County would be having a new sheriff if Emily Covenay wasn't recovered safe and well.

'You think you can wriggle off the hook with your smooth words,' said Jackson contemptuously. 'Don't think it for a moment. What good turn could you do me? Come on, get dressed. We got a long ride ahead of us in a few hours.'

Rick O'Shea didn't stir, but said instead: 'First off is where I was coming through the Gap because the priest back in San Angelo asked me to help him. It was chance alone that brought me there when those fools were after blowing up the railroad train.'

'Father Flaherty? What's your connection with him?'

'I'm Catholic. I was talking to the father, day before yesterday, and he told me of the terrible plight of a fellow Catholic: Mr Covenay.'

'Tom Covenay? You talking about the theft of his child?'

O'Shea could see that he had the sheriff's attention now and no mistake. It was only a question of reeling him in. It wouldn't do, though, to let Jackson think that he, Rick O'Shea, was acting under duress. His best bet was to represent himself as voluntarily offering to rescue the little girl.

'We Catholics stand by each other,

Sheriff,' O'Shea said. 'Soon as I heard of this awful business I resolved at once to do all I could. I offered my services to Father Flaherty and — well — here I am.'

Sheriff Jackson said nothing for a space, mulling over what he had been told. At length he said:

'What's this to me? You talked of a good turn; how does that work?'

'Why, man, I've no wish for any glory in this affair. I'd be happy for you to take all the credit for bringing the child safely back to the bosom of her family. We'll work in tandem, as you might say, then I'll be happy just to see the child back home. You can tell everybody as how you did it all by your own self. Do you a power of good when the election's held, I'll be bound.'

'There's more to the case than you're letting on, O'Shea, of that I've no doubt. Still and all, there might be something in it. Father Flaherty, he'd back up what you say, would he? Don't bother lying to me, now.'

'I was with him for half an hour, day before yesterday, a little after noon. He'll confirm that.'

'I'm telling you, you better not be lying to me,' said Sheriff Jackson in a threatening tone of voice. He may not have been quite as agile and sharp mentally as Rick O'Shea, but he had already run through the angles in his mind. He had the train robbers, or what was left of them, in the bag, and he had aimed anyway to bring home little Emily Covenay. Set against that, just adding one more name to the train-wreckers already in custody would profit him nothing. He uncocked his piece with his thumb and slipped it back into the holster.

'Tell me what you got in mind,' he said.

3

Since neither man completely trusted the other, by tacit consent Jackson and O'Shea chose to abandon sleep for the night. As it was only a couple of hours until dawn they left the poky little room and went down to the deserted riverbank to talk over the best way of proceeding. As they strolled through the empty streets O'Shea said:

'I'm guessing that you know as Yanez is at the back of the business?'

'The devil he is!' replied Jackson. 'Who told you so?'

'Ah, I can't reveal my sources, Sheriff.'

'You better had,' said Jackson, stopping dead in his tracks and staring hard at O'Shea.

'Since you put it so, it was Father Flaherty his own self who gave me the tip.'

'What does he know about it? I find he's been holding out on information relating to this matter and I'm going to be mighty vexed with that priest.'

'He *is* a priest. It's the kind of thing they get to know. I'll warrant he knows more secrets than a prostitute's dog, that one.'

'I suppose it comes of hearing all those confessions.'

This was not an angle that Rick O'Shea wished to explore, so he changed the subject.

'You got no jurisdiction away over the river, I dare say?'

'Not a bit,' replied the sheriff cheerfully. 'But that don't bother me none. I been over there in the past, bringing back fugitives and such. The government in Mexico City don't mind. They'd be glad to see Yanez given a black eye and made to look foolish.'

O'Shea shot a quick glance at his companion.

'We ain't aiming for to give anybody a black eye, are we?' he said. 'Just bringing that child safely home.'

'Ain't even said yet that there is any 'we' in the case. If we do act together though, I wouldn't mind causing some harm to Yanez in the process. I owe him a bad turn.'

They breakfasted in a little cantina on the water-front, which began serving meals as soon as dawn broke. It was agreed that the two of them would cross over on the ferry that afternoon, after gathering a few provisions. Jackson was not a sociable companion, whereas Rick O'Shea was always in the mood for chatting away about this and that. Halfway through their meal, Sheriff Jackson said abruptly:

'You talk more'n a woman, you know that?'

'Sure — and what's the purpose in being alive if we can't enjoy ourselves and so forth?'

'Beats me,' said Jackson. 'I suppose we're stuck here with it. Until we die, that is.'

'That's the hell of a gloomy way of

looking at life, you know. Look at me now. I take things as they come, as you might say.'

'Yes and you take other folks' belongings as they come as well, O'Shea. It's not a way of life I'd care for. Listen, there's one thing always puzzled me about you. Is Rick O'Shea your real name or is it an alias? It's a strange coincidence, living as an outlaw and having a name that sounds just like 'ricochet', you'll have to allow.'

'I'll tell you the truth of it. Back home — in the old country, I mean — I was known as Dick, in the English fashion, my given name being Richard. But it sounded not quite the thing here to be calling meself Dick, if you take my meaning. Not so dignified, so I came up with 'Rick O'Shea'. You have to admit it suits me well enough.'

Sheriff Jackson grunted and turned his attention back to his coffee. Rick O'Shea realized that riding with Jackson was not going to be a bunch of laughs, by any stretch of the imagination. In the usual way of things O'Shea got on well enough with lawmen. Indeed, he often found that he had more in common with them than he did with ordinary citizens. Villains and lawmen were both playing the same game in many respects, although of course being, nominally at least, on opposing teams. They played by rules of whose very existence the average law-abiding person was unaware, and both sides worked according to a set of cynical assumptions that would perhaps have shocked most people.

At the back of his mind Rick O'Shea had half-thought that a trip across the border like this, working together with a sheriff, might prove to be quite a diverting and entertaining affair. With anybody other than an out-and-out stiff 'un such as Seth Jackson, that might indeed have been the case. As it was, he was seemingly destined to embark upon this enterprise with one of the dullest and most humourless men who ever drew breath. Well, so be it!

Once the stores in the little town had opened Jackson and O'Shea gathered together some provisions for their expedition. It was obviously necessary that they should travel light, so they limited themselves to food and to powder and shot for their weapons. The two of them agreed that in addition to these necessities several other useful items such as a coil of rope and one or two other bits and pieces might come in handy.

Even as they prepared for crossing the river later that day Sheriff Jackson did not once make the rules of play clear by assuring O'Shea that he would not at some future time arrest him for his supposed involvement in the ambush of the train. The question lay unspoken between them and Rick O'Shea took it as read that the sheriff's intention was to keep him in a state of constant uneasiness regarding his future prospects.

For his own part, as soon as he had

rescued the little girl and restored her to her family O'Shea had no intention at all of waiting around in or near San Angelo to see what the sheriff's pleasure might be. He would be off to New York at once and if anybody tried to hinder him, then so much the worse for them.

The fellow operating the ferry did not run his service according to any particular schedule, but took men and goods across as and when required. He charged varying amounts, according to what he perceived to be the personal risk to himself and his livelihood. If he were to be caught shifting arms across the border he might reasonably expect to suffer some penalty, along with those in actual possession of the weaponry. He had a quick eye for wrongdoing and was generally able to gauge quickly enough how much his services were worth to a potential customer, and also to assess the possible hazard that he would be exposed to if the thing miscarried.

Although Sheriff Jackson had removed his badge he was well enough known to one or two people in Archangel, who had made sure to spread the word to all the town that they were being favoured with a visit by the law. So it was that when Jackson and O'Shea fetched up at the ferry that afternoon, the owner regretfully informed them that he was unable to oblige because he was that day undertaking vital repairs to the raft.

'Don't jerk me around,' said Sheriff Jackson irritably when told this. 'I saw you taking three men over earlier this very day. What do you mean by it?'

The man shrugged apologetically.

'Cable's fouled. It ain't my fault. Not apt to be fixed for at least a week. I'm sorry an' all, but there it is.'

O'Shea watched this exchange and observed the sheriff's rising anger with amusement. He understood just as well as Sheriff Jackson what was behind this little piece of play-acting: namely that the ferryman knew that when a sheriff required some service the money would be coming not from his private resources, but would rather be drawn from the public purse. That being so it was surely worth doubling or even trebling what he would have charged a private individual for a similar trip.

There was something delightfully entertaining about the situation, not least for various loafers who were hanging around the landing stage with nothing better to do than watch a much-loathed lawman having his tail twisted and being in no position to do a damned thing about it. Jackson could hardly announce officially that he was the sheriff of Pecos County and was about to enter a neighbouring country where he had no business operating. This was meant to be a clandestine mission and the longer he delayed here the more chance there was of people asking what he was up to.

In the end, he offered three times as much as the journey was worth, which had the immediate effect of freeing up the 'fouled cable' and allowing the trip to begin.

There had been some debate before setting off for the ferry as to whether Jackson and O'Shea should take their horses with them or leave them in Archangel. If the distance to Chuchuverical had been greater O'Shea would have been all for ensuring that they had the means to travel fast but, as he set out the matter to Jackson, the village was only a mile or two from the river and they could walk it in under an hour. Since their own hope of success lay in concealment, walking quietly through the rocky landscape that surrounded the village would perhaps offer more hope for their purposes than thundering towards their target on horseback. When all was said and done, their best chance lay in secrecy rather than in force of arms.

Once they had been landed on the Mexican shore the two men set off at a tangent, heading south-east rather than directly south towards Chuchuverical. There were other Anglos about, so they did not really stick out to any great degree. As they strolled in this circuitous route towards Chuchuverical, O'Shea remarked:

'Who would have imagined you and me, Sheriff, making common cause in this way?'

'I ain't making common cause with you. Don't think it for a moment. I got no interest in you, O'Shea, other than how useful you can be to me.'

'You're a hard man to like, you know that?'

'I don't want that you should like me. I'd say I'd gone down the wrong road somewhere were I to find that a thief like you was to get to liking me.'

'Well, have it so. I was only after making conversation.'

'Well, don't. I don't like you, O'Shea, and the good Lord help you if ever I find that you been leading me out here on a snipe hunt.'

'Why would I be doing such a thing as that?'

'I couldn't say,' said Sheriff Jackson. 'I wouldn't put anything past you.'

They walked on in uncomfortable silence for another half-mile, then O'Shea said:

'You know about this compound of Yanez's that I heard about?'

'I heard tell of it.'

'You ever been there?'

'What's that supposed to mean?'

Rick O'Shea glanced sideways at the sheriff, puzzled.

'I got the impression from what you said that you'd been over this way before,' he said. 'Just wondered if you'd had reason to pass this village and maybe knew aught about Yanez's hideout. Nothing more.'

'Oh, I see what you mean. Yeah, I seen it from a distance.'

O'Shea's face took on a slightly puzzled look.

'What did you think I meant?' he asked.

'Happen I told you before, O'Shea, I ain't wishing to chat with you like you're some old friend that I was at school with. Let's you and me just get on with the job in hand and not pretend that we like each other overmuch.'

Their path led them up on to the slopes of a steep hill, which overlooked the village of Chuchuverical. The ground was covered in scree with many large boulders and rocks lying on the loose stones and drifts of grit. This meant that they had no difficulty in approaching the village without being seen. Unless somebody in the village were to be training a pair of field glasses straight in their direction, the odds were a hundred to one against anybody down below seeing the two figures as they picked their way across the dusty incline.

'Let's halt awhiles and see what's to do next,' Sheriff Jackson suggested.

When they were sitting among the rocks, partially obscured from view of anybody in the village beneath them, Jackson pointed a finger:

'See over yonder? Those white walls, a bit beyond the other buildings? That's Yanez's compound. I'd guess that that's where he's holding the child.'

O'Shea studied the place for a spell.

'If those walls are just adobe,' he said, 'then cracking 'em open with a couple o' pounds of fine-grain powder would be the easiest thing in the world. Howsoever, easily in, but not so easily out again, as the lobster said when it found its way into the pot. It's not just Yanez's men as'd be after us. I've a notion that every man in that village would turn out to catch the Anglos and show 'em whose country they're in.'

'Trust an Irishman to think of blowing something up. Your Fenian tricks won't serve here, O'Shea. We'll be needing a little subtlety.'

'And if it's subtlety you're wanting, you can't do better than go to Seth Jackson's shop, is that the way of it? Well, what do ye recommend?'

'For now,' Jackson replied, 'I recommend that we settle down here and have us a little siesta, until dusk. Then you'll see what I have in mind.'

'Why the blazes did we cross over so early,' asked O'Shea with some asperity, 'if we're going to waste our time now just sitting and doing nothing? We could have done nothing in Archangel for a few hours.'

'Listen, I can get us in there, where Yanez is based. What's more, I've a shrewd idea that I know where in the place he's holding that poor child.'

'The hell you do!' exclaimed Rick O'Shea in astonishment. 'Why didn't you say so before?'

'You ever ask yourself why the Lord gave us one mouth and two ears? So as we can listen twice as much as we speak. Never you mind what I know and what I don't know. The two of us together'll get that child back. Trust me.'

If his life had taught Rick O'Shea anything at all, then two lessons about human nature stood out clearly in his mind. The first was that when a man says: *It's not what it looks like* it invariably is. The other was that whenever anybody says: Trust me, then that is the last thing on God's Earth that you should be doing. He didn't say any of this to Sheriff Jackson, but simply shrugged and settled back with his hat over his face to see what would happen next.

After having his sleep disturbed the night before and being awake since about three in the morning, O'Shea found it even easier than usual to be able to fall instantly asleep. When he was woken by Sheriff Jackson with a sharp prod in his ribs from the sheriff's boot it was dark and the silver sliver of a nearly new moon, no thicker than a nail-paring, hung in the night sky.

'Get up, you lazy Irisher. You been slumbering like a hog. We got work to do.'

It had not escaped O'Shea's notice that ever since they had arrived on the

Mexican side of the border Jackson had taken to acting as though he were in command and this whole thing were his very own show. This was a little strange, since as far as O'Shea understood the matter the whole scheme of coming across here to snatch back the child had been his idea entirely. He mentioned nothing of these doubts.

'Well, what's to do?' he asked, sitting up.

'We're going over to that compound, that's what to do. We'll carry on walking the long way round, staying in the shadows so that we're not marked. Once we get within striking distance I'll tell you what my plan is.'

'Could you not be telling me now?'

'No,' said Sheriff Jackson in a voice that did not invite further discussion.

The two men walked along without talking, making their way to the wall of Yanez's compound that faced away from the village of Chuchuverical. There did not appear to be anybody about, although judging by the height of the moon in the sky it was still early evening. When they reached the lime-washed adobe wall, which was perhaps ten feet high, Sheriff Jackson spoke to O'Shea in a soft voice:

'Go feel the wall there; you see where that crack is?'

Hugely puzzled, Rick O'Shea walked forward a few paces and reached out his hand to touch the wall. It felt slightly rough, but there was nothing out of the ordinary about it that he could make out. While he was doing this, Sheriff Jackson stepped forward and, while removing O'Shea's pistol from its holster, drew his own and pointed it at the other man's back.

'You really are one stupid son of a bitch,' he said. 'You know that?'

O'Shea turned round. Seeing that he had a gun pointing at him he immediately reached down for his own weapon, knowing as he did so that it was probably not going to be there. The sheriff gave a piercing series of whistles, presumably a code or password of some kind. Then he spoke to O'Shea.

'Come on you, round to the front door. I know Yanez will be glad to see you. How he'll laugh when I tell him the story of how you thought that you were persuading me to come here.'

Feeling like the biggest fool since the world's creation, O'Shea walked ahead of Sheriff Jackson round to the front of the little fortlike construction. The main gate was open. Standing there, illuminated by the light of two blazing pine knots held by the men who accompanied him, his face split with a broad smile, was the man who, O'Shea figured, could only be Valentin Yanez.

'Jackson, my friend,' said Yanez, 'it surely is good to see you again. And what's this? You've brought me a present?'

'Let me introduce the famous Rick O'Shea,' announced Jackson mockingly. 'The man who's going to provide the finishing touch to all our plans.'

4

Wondering how he could have been so careless in overlooking so many clues as to the true nature of the enterprise in which he had been engaged, Rick O'Shea found himself being prodded forward at gunpoint and compelled to enter Yanez's compound. Once they were all within the courtyard the gate was closed and barred. O'Shea stopped dead and turned to face Jackson.

'You're a damned villain,' he said, 'worse than any bandit I ever heard tell of.'

By way of answer Sheriff Jackson swung the pistol in his hand across O'Shea's face, splitting his lips, loosening a couple of teeth and sending him sprawling to the ground.

'Any more such words from you,' said Jackson quietly, 'I'll kill you straight off and to hell with the consequences.'

O'Shea had no reason at all to believe that the sheriff was speaking anything other than the literal truth. He accordingly remained silent and waited to see what would develop. It was Yanez who broke the tension between the two of them.

'Ah, you cannot let this man go to his death without knowing *why* he must die,' he remarked. 'That would be too cruel, even by my standards.'

Jackson shrugged and scowled, but the Mexican did not take the hint. He continued:

'I don't know how the good sheriff here managed to lure you to my home — '

At this point Sheriff Jackson burst into laughter.

'Lure him?' he said. 'The boot's on the other foot entirely. It was him who was so all-fired up to come and visit you, Yanez. I only obliged him by showing him the way. It was all his doing.'

By the light of the pine torches

O'Shea was able to study Yanez's face and found that it was a deal more pleasing than that of the crooked sheriff. There was, it was true, cruelty and animal passion, but these traits were mingled with good humour and intelligence. It was by no means an unlikable countenance. Yanez looked down at where O'Shea was lying, then unexpectedly bent down and stretched out his hand to help him to his feet.

'Your sheriff,' explained Yanez, once Rick O'Shea was standing again, 'is my friend. We work together. He helps me and I help him. We have a saying in Spanish which translates as 'One hand washes the other'. When my friend became aware that he might not be re-elected, there was consternation. Not only for him, but for me too. Imagine! What would happen if I found myself dealing with an honest sheriff on the other side of the Rio? No, it would never do.

'So we hatch a plan, he and I. One which keeps him in his job, which is to my advantage and also pays me — how much was it again?' he turned to Sheriff Jackson.

'Five thousand dollars.'

'Five thousand?' asked O'Shea. 'The figure I heard was ten.'

Yanez smile widened even further.

'Ten was what your sheriff told me to put in the ransom note,' he said, 'but we neither of us expected to get that.'

'For all that Tom dresses up fine for church on Sundays,' Jackson said, 'those Covenays are poor as they come. Putting on airs and graces when he's no wealthier than me. I think I see us getting ten thousand dollars out of that family.'

That both Sheriff Jackson and the Mexican were being so forthcoming about their innermost secrets was not encouraging. O'Shea simply couldn't see how Jackson could possibly allow him to live after what he had been privy to this evening.

'Where do I fit in to all this?' he asked.

'Well now,' said Yanez affably, 'I was surprised when the sheriff arrived with you, but I see at once what he is about. You are to be our . . . how do you call it in English? Ah yes — the 'fall- guy'.' He turned to Jackson. 'Am I right? Is that both the correct expression and tells me what brings you here with this fellow?'

'Both right.'

Yanez turned courteously back to Rick O'Shea.

'You see,' he continued, 'having abstracted this child from her home and secreted her here in my own country, we both needed to turn a profit on the business — and also benefit my friend here: to make sure that he was confirmed as sheriff for at least another year. A newspaper with connections back East has offered a reward of no less than five thousand dollars for the safe return of the little girl, coupled with the arrest of the perpetrator.'

In spite of his detestation of this type of crime, O'Shea couldn't help feeling a slight admiration for such a neatly contructed plot.

'I wonder that the paper didn't just offer to pay the ransom for the child straight to the men who stole her away,' he said.

'Wouldn't be legal,' said Sheriff Jackson at once. 'That'd be what we call compounding a felony.'

'And so,' Yanez said, wrapping it up, 'our friend Jackson will bring the rescued child back to San Angelo and confirm that one of my men was instrumental in solving the case. He will then be able to collect the reward money. Unless I am greatly mistaken, you will play the part of the bandit himself. Killed, I am guessing, while resisting lawful arrest. Am I right?' He turned again to Jackson, who nodded.

'The citizens,' Yanez went on, 'will be so impressed by their sheriff's courage and tenacity that they will wish to keep him, in addition to which he gains a thousand dollars. I and my men will have four thousand and everybody will be happy. It is a sound plan, no?'

'The only loser seems likely to be me,' observed O'Shea. 'From what I can make out, I am apt to be killed before this little comedy reaches its end.'

'That is so,' said Yanez regretfully. 'But such are the fortunes of life. We will at least feed you well during your stay here.'

'Yes,' Jackson put in, 'I want him alive at least 'til we cross the river again. It'll be no good me carting back some stinking corpse and trying to make out I just shot him. I'll wait until we're nigh to San Angelo.'

The Mexican bandit was one thing, a crooked sheriff something else again; Rick O'Shea resolved at that moment that whatever else befell him, he would see Seth Jackson in his grave before this affair was ended. In the meantime, his wrists were lashed behind his back with a rawhide thong and he was taken to a small shed that was used to store tack for the horses. There he was left to reflect upon his fate.

It was not the first tight spot that O'Shea had been in in his life and he had no reason at all to believe that it would be the last. Yanez, for all his cunning, could not help boasting about how clever he was being and that had given his captive something of an edge. The knowledge that those devils meant to kill him out of hand meant that O'Shea had absolutely nothing to lose.

He didn't doubt his ability to break free of his present predicament; the only debatable point was whether or not he would be able to do so and live for more than a minute or two afterwards. In other circumstances he might perhaps have bided his time and waited for something to present itself, but if he was going to be killed in any case — well then, there was no use sitting and waiting for the end to come.

The first thing to attend to were his bonds. It is amazing how even quite intelligent and experienced men will sometimes tie a fellow's hands behind his back and think that they have thus rendered him entirely helpless. In fact, any reasonably lithe and agile person can easily slip the bound hands over his buttocks and then, by drawing up his knees to his chest, slide them also over his feet. With the bonds now on the wrists in front of him it is a poor fish who is unable to work a few knots loose with his teeth. It takes time, but it is not overly difficult to accomplish.

Within twenty minutes Rick O'Shea had his hands free and was thus at liberty to turn his attention to escaping from the little outbuilding in which he was confined. The two small windows were not barred, but O'Shea doubted that he would have been able to wriggle his way through the tiny squares. They were barely twelve inches wide and high up on the wall; their only purpose being to let in a little light. The door was stout and looked as though it would resist any amount of kicking; not that he really wanted to be kicking up a shindy and advertising his attempts to bust out. There remained but one option.

On more than one occasion in the past O'Shea had found himself being held in little lock-ups, one of which had been even smaller than this. Not all little towns ran to a proper jail built into the back of the sheriff's office; sometimes drunks and other minor lawbreakers were shoved into a tiny outbuilding like this for a couple of days.

It was during one such spell of temporary incarceration that Rick O'Shea had discovered an interesting fact: that however strong windows and doors might be, most buildings had one weak spot; this was the roof.

When you stick a roof on anywhere, whether it be a house, barn, shed or privy, you are more concerned with making sure that the wind does not blow it off than you are likely to worry about some fool pushing at it from within. Who would ever do such a thing? The roof of the little place where O'Shea was being held was barely seven feet from the ground. He swept a harness and some tools from a heavy table, then hopped up on to it, almost banging his head on the roof beam in the process. Then he bent down and pressed his back against the beam and began pushing upwards.

Almost at once he felt movement, but then he immediately stopped. There had been a screeching of nails as they protested at being wrenched free. Before making his move O'Shea would have to be sure that there was nobody in the vicinity who would be alarmed by the sight and sound of a roof rising into the air. He got down from the table and dragged it over to one of the tiny windows.

It was almost completely dark now and from the window O'Shea was able to get some sense of the shed's surroundings. The compound in which the shed stood covered an area of an acre or so. This was enclosed by an adobe wall too high to be climbed without assistance. In the centre of the compound stood an imposing house that looked more like a New Orleans townhouse than anything else that Rick O'Shea had ever seen. Its appearance here, near to the modest little village of single-storey dwellings was, to O'Shea's mind, more than a little incongruous. Plainly, Valentin Yanez was riding high on the hog and wasn't ashamed to let everybody know it.

In addition to the house there looked to be a half-dozen other, smaller buildings: stables and sheds by the look of them. There was nobody about as far as O'Shea could see. Judging from the lights and sound of laughter and loud voices from the house Yanez and his boys were making merry. This was all to the good.

It was unlikely that anybody would be worrying their heads about him until the morning. As far as they were concerned he was safely tucked away in here, where he could do no harm. This was good, because it meant that there need be no great rush to do anything.

O'Shea stood and examined the table critically, then hopped up again to look at the wall surrounding Yanez's lair.

The table stood about three feet high and the wall outside was no more than eight feet high. Why, it should be child's play if, once out of the shed, he was able to push this table up to the wall, jump up and scramble over it. Then he suddenly recollected with a shock that he had no way of getting the table to the wall, on account of what but the door was locked. The resolution to this puzzle, when it came, was simplicity itself.

The window at the front showed pretty much the whole of Yanez's little realm. It might be worth, thought O'Shea, looking to see what was to be seen out back. He hauled the table over to the other window, climbed up and was delighted to find that the rear wall of the shed in which he was presently confined was no more than three feet from the wall around the compound. Why, there was nothing to stop him leaving this minute!

There would without doubt be some kind of pursuit when it was found that he had gone; for one thing, that fool Jackson had told him altogether too much about his crooked affairs to be able to risk O'Shea getting back to Pecos County. Well then, it wouldn't be the first time that Rick O'Shea had played the part of quarry in a hunt and here he still was, large as life and twice as natural. He'd do well enough.

There seemed to be no reason to delay his departure. O'Shea, after having one last look out the front to check that the coast was clear, moved the table to the back of the shed, climbed up and applied his strength to the roof there, pushing upwards with all his might. There was less noise this time, perhaps because some of the nails had already been loosened, and he found that the roof was prised loose of the top of the walls in no time.

He shifted it sideways, leaving it propped on top of the little building at a strange angle, then scrambled through the gap until he was perched on the rear wall, where the roof had lately been resting. Then he leaped towards the high adobe wall behind and was able to lower himself from there to the ground outside without any great difficulty.

He then set off at a brisk pace for the foothills of the mountains that loomed above the village of Chuchuverical.

By O'Shea's calculations he need not fear any attempt at pursuit before dawn. His reasoning was that the men he had heard in the big house sounded to him to have been in the early stages of intoxication. It was ten to one against their bothering about him that night. The chances were that they would not even notice that the roof of the shed was a bit skew-wiff. Even if they did, would they think it profitable to come haring out into the darkness to try and track him down? It would be madness; they'd surely wait until first light. All this having been considered, he slowed down a little as he gained the hills and prepared to pace himself in his efforts to reach the mountains by sunrise.

So occupied was Rick O'Shea with his plans and so self-satisfied was he with his cleverness in having freed himself from the coils of what could have been a very nasty situation, that he wasn't paying all that much heed to his present surroundings. Which was why it wasn't until he was right on top of him, that he all but stumbled in the darkness over a young man who was lying on the ground and sighting down a rifle. This person, when once he knew that O'Shea was aware of his presence, pulled out a pistol, stood up slowly and said:

'You come a step closer and I'll shoot you down like a dog.'

This was such an unlooked-for development that O'Shea was for a moment at a loss to know how to proceed. He played for time.

'Whoa there,' he said, 'there's no need for that at all.' As he spoke, his mind was working hard as could be, trying to work out the play. Was this some sentry set here by Yanez to guard his stronghold? Or was he just some bandit who happened to be in the area? Then, cursing himself for being such a slow-witted dullard, O'Shea thought to himself that the most curious circumstance of all was that this young fellow was speaking not Spanish but English.

O'Shea stood stock still, for when somebody's drawing down on you with a pistol the last thing you wish to do is make some terrible mistake that can never be set right in this world. He tried to reduce tension a notch or two. 'You ain't a Mexican, surely?' he said. 'What're you up to here?'

'Never you mind what I'm up to,' said the boy with great firmness. 'I might ask you the self-same question, if it comes to that. You come up here seeking me?'

'Seeking you? I'm not after seeking anything, other than to be away from this place. I've no quarrel with you that I know of. Will you let me pass?'

The youth said nothing for a spell, then asked:

'You come from down yonder?'

The more he heard the boy speak the more O'Shea began to think that there was something not quite right about him. When he figured what it was, despite his perilous predicament Rick O'Shea laughed out loud.

'What's so funny?' asked the youth fiercely. 'Don't think as you can push me around.'

'You're no boy,' said O'Shea. 'What in the name of all that's wonderful is a young girl doing up here with a rifle and pistol?'

'I ain't so young as all that. I'm nineteen.'

'Mother of God! You say you're nineteen? Don't tell me you're after being Emily Covenay's sister?'

'Well, and what of it? You best don't forget I still got the drop on you. You ain't even carrying. You needn't think I'd hesitate to shoot, neither.'

'I believe you well enough, but it'll

not be needful, d'ye see? Why, we're on the same side entirely.'

The young woman, for now that he had heard the confirmation from her lips, he could see at once that this was the case, said:

'The same side? I don't rightly understand you. What side you talking about?'

'Why, getting your sister out of here and back home with you and your pa. What else?' It looked to O'Shea as if the young person was inclined to argue the point and make difficulties. He went on:

'I just escaped from where your sister's being held, but I mean to go back for her. But for now I'd feel better if we could move further from Yanez's place. I'll walk ahead of you if it'll make you fell safer, but for the love of God let's be moving higher up this slope.'

The woman gave the matter some thought, then said:

'Are you a lawman?'

'Not a bit of it.'

'You're Irish, I know that much.'

'Sure and what of it?'

'Nothing. My pa's Irish as well.'

'Very interesting, but can we just be making tracks now?'

The woman picked up a heavy-looking pack and put the pistol back in a holster which she had rigged under her arm. Then she picked up the rifle.

'You're not a Mexican bandit,' she said, 'I know that much. Maybe I can trust you.'

The two of them set off up the scree-covered slope, which led towards the mountains. O'Shea found that he was making heavy weather of the climb, but the young woman seemingly took it in her stride. It had been quite dark earlier, but now the clouds slid away revealing a gibbous moon, which shed its pale and meagre light upon the scene. Now that he could see her, which he did by stealing surreptitious glances at intervals, it was obvious that this was a young woman who had simply hacked off her long hair and donned a man's clothes. Her hair was ragged and unkempt and O'Shea guessed that she had simply chopped it off with the kitchen scissors.

He noticed that the rifle she was toting under her arm was of a strange design.

'That's a mighty odd-looking weapon you have there. You know how to use it?'

'I can shoot better than you, most likely.'

The further they went the steeper was the slope and the looser and more heavy-going was the scree. The good thing was that they were now out of sight of Yanez's little fort; tracking anybody through this grit and dust would be an arduous task, assuming that those chasing him didn't have a pack of blood-hounds at their disposal. The young woman didn't seem even to be breaking sweat, but O'Shea was beginning to gasp with the effort. At last he stopped dead in his tracks.

'Would you be halting for a minute or

two, missy?' he pleaded.

The woman whirled round like a cat. 'I'll thank you not to call me 'miss',' she said. 'Strikes me that you're out of condition that a little stroll like this should leave you panting like an old horse, ready for the knacker's yard.'

O'Shea stared at her, unable to decide whether he was angry or amused.

'And haven't you got a mouth on you, then,' she said. 'If you're not the law, what's your interest in rescuing my sister?'

'It's a penance,' O'Shea replied, not seeing the need to conceal the fact from this forthright young woman. Besides which, it would at least show her that he was to be trusted. After all, the Covenays were Catholics too and she would likely understand such a thing. 'The priest back in San Angelo, Father Flaherty is it? He set me off on this little trip.'

The girl looked at him dubiously.

'Didn't Father Flaherty tell me that

he'd been praying hard and that the Lord would provide?' she said. 'Mind, I should have thought He might have done better than a man who can't walk up a hill without getting winded, but I guess it can't be helped.'

'Well then, would you like me to go back to my home and leave you waiting for the Lord to send you an archangel with a burning sword or something of the sort?' asked O'Shea, irritated. 'If, that is, you're not after being satisfied with what's on offer.'

'I guess you'll have to do. Tell me what you know of this business.'

As briefly as possible Rick O'Shea outlined the steps in his pilgrimage up until that moment. The woman mulled over what he said, then dismissed his trials and tribulation by casually observing:

'You don't seem to have accomplished a single thing. It's a good job I came myself. So Sheriff Jackson's a rogue, is he? That's news, at any rate.'

'I suppose you'd have done better,

would you?' O'Shea said, stung by her attitude.

'I couldn't have done worse,' she replied. 'Let's carry on up to that pine wood there.'

Fuming inwardly yet at the same time conceding that she had a point, O'Shea continued up the slope alongside the woman. He couldn't yet make up his mind whether bumping into this young person was a tremendous stroke of good fortune or a damned nuisance.

5

Neither O'Shea nor the woman felt inclined to sleep: it was only the evening. Once he had given her a somewhat fuller account of his adventures she apparently realized that they would both need to be on the alert, for it was impossible to say when Yanez and the sheriff would be coming to find their escaped prisoner. When he had finished detailing the sequence of events that had brought him to this point, O'Shea asked tentatively what the story was behind the young woman's presence on the hill overlooking Chuchuverical.

'The truth is,' she told him, 'I didn't trust to anybody else to find my sister and bring her safely home. Sheriff Jackson don't exactly inspire one with confidence, even without knowing he's crooked. So I got some of the men on our place — the hands and such, you understand, to ask around. They heard a rumour that a man called Yanez was behind it. I'd never so much as heard the name until that moment.

'Then I went to Father Flaherty and told him I was going to go off searching for Emily. I let him think that he was talking me out of the idea and I picked up some more clues from him, though he didn't tell me all he knew, that's for sure.'

'Tell me you didn't travel all the way here on your own?' said O'Shea, aghast.

'Well then, I did. All the way to Archangel, where I paid some scamp to point out across the river where Yanez had his base; then I took the ferry across the river and here I am.'

'Why, it's sheer madness! What was your father thinking of, letting it happen?'

'You tend to your own affairs and leave me to look after my own,' she said tartly. 'I can take care of myself well enough.'

'At least you'll allow that it'd be crazy for us to work separately. We'd be tripping over each other and like as not end up shooting each other by accident.'

Neither then nor later did Rick O'Shea manage to elicit from the woman precisely what her plans had been for recovering her sister safely. From all that he was able to collect, she had come up to the hills above Chuchuverical and, apart from peering down at the place through the telescope on her rifle, had little idea what to do next to achieve her object.

The gun that she was toting was of a curious design; one that O'Shea had never encountered.

'Would you be minding if I had a look-see at that musket of yours?' he said, 'I never seen the like.'

Jemima Covenay handed the rifle to O'Shea. He hefted it in his hands.

'My, but that weighs more than I'd be wanting to carry round with me,' he said. 'And what's this little tube on the top supposed to do?'

'It's a telescope sight. This is a Whitworth. My pa carried it all through the war; he was a sharpshooter. They called these here 'widowmakers', on account of men with one o' these hardly ever missed their mark.'

'You a tolerable good shot with it? Looks a right ungainly piece of ordnance for a girl to be using.'

'I been firing this since I was ten. My pa, he was never to have a son, so I took that part. Used to go hunting with him from when I was knee-high to a grasshopper. My ma, God rest her, she weren't none too happy, but Pa's a man who'll have his own way. I can kill anything as moves with this, up to a thousand yards.'

'Can ye, now? You ever kill a man?'

'Not yet, but before God, I see the man that took our Emily away and I'll pull the trigger on him and not think twice on it.'

O'Shea looked at the girl in frank admiration.

'By God,' he said, 'I believe you! But before anything of that sort, we've to be finding where that sister o' yourn is stowed. Happen there'll be time for vengeance afterwards.'

Jemima Covenay looked at O'Shea with an air of contempt.

'Well, I found that out just an hour or so afore you came blundering up here.'

'You know where the child is? Mother o' God! Why have ye not said so before now?'

'Weren't sure of you 'til now, that's why. But now, having heard that you know Father Flaherty and all, I reckon as you're all right, least in this matter.'

The coolness of the young woman surpassed all belief. Never in his life had Rick O'Shea heard a person of this age speak with such calm self-assurance. Despite the desperation of their situation, he was enchanted.

'Well,' he said, 'this isn't business. Where's this precious sister of yours being held? In Yanez's compound, I've no doubt.'

'Not a bit of it. I was looking down at yon village through my sights — this telescope, I mean, and I saw Emily walking along the little street there.'

'How'd she seem? Was she distressed or harmed or aught of that nature?'

'The opposite. She was skipping along merrily beside this old woman, looked to be chattering away like she'd not a care in the world.'

'That's rummy! I'd o' thought she would have been scared out of her wits to be taken away from her home and carried away here to a place where they speak another language.'

Jemima Covenay said nothing for a space, but stared straight out into the darkness. At length, she spoke.

'I suppose,' she said slowly, 'there's something I should mention. My sister's the darlingest thing, but she ain't overly endowed in the brains department, if you take my meaning.'

'What are you saying? She's simple?'

'She's a natural. I doubt she'll go far in this world without me and Pa to look after her. She's fey, away with the fairies much o' the time.'

Now it was O'Shea's turn to keep silent for a while. He thought what a foul crime this was. Taking a little girl away was bad enough, but one who was not right in the head? Who would be so wicked as to undertake a crime like that? He had already decided that he and Seth Jackson would be having a reckoning, but it was at this point that O'Shea knew that he would be killing any of those he could get his hands on who had been a part of this monstrous plot.

'So you saw your sister,' he said. 'What then?'

'This 'scope magnifies by four. I could see 'most every detail and the two of them, the woman and Emily, went into the last house at the edge of the village. They didn't come out again, so I'm thinking that she's staying there.'

'You say you're a dab hand with the rifle; what about that pistol?'

'Not so good.'

'If you're game and will let me have the loan of that gun at your hip, we can go down this minute and try and get your sister. That is to say, I'll do what's needful and you can stand guard.'

The girl snorted in derision.

'Don't think it for a moment,' she said. 'You want the lending of this pistol, then we work together.'

'Lord, but you're a tough one! All right, let's get down to the village. I've not seen any disturbance yet, so I'm guessing that they've yet to find me gone.'

The walk down the slope back to Chuchuverical was a lot easier for O'Shea than the ascent had been. As they went along he tried to unravel the situation out loud.

'I heard that Yanez has family in Chuchuverical. I mind as he's let some female relative take care of your sister. It's a mercy that she didn't seem to you to be upset.'

'You think that makes it right?'

'No, by God! I think it's the wickedest thing I ever heard of in my life. There'll be a reckoning for this, but I want you and the little girl safely out of the way first.'

By the time O'Shea and the girl were within earshot of Yanez's walled compound they could plainly hear the sound of drunken merrymaking. The village of Chuchuverical, on the other hand, looked and sounded as quiet as the tomb. There were not even any lights showing in windows. Presumably, thought O'Shea, these men were farmers and worked on the general principle of early to bed and early to rise.

Once they were on the level ground O'Shea spoke again.

'Will you be letting me have that gunbelt now?'

Jemima Covenay unbuckled the rig and handed it to him, remarking as she did so:

'There's an empty chamber under the hammer. It's single action, you know. You needs must cock it before firing.'

'Let's hope it don't come to that.'

Once he was carrying a gun again O'Shea felt more as though he were able to tackle things.

'If you think that you can kill a man,' he said, 'then I'd be mighty obliged for you to take up position here, by the corner of that house, and cover Yanez's abode. I'd feel safer knowing as somebody was guarding my back. If you see anybody coming from the compound and definitely heading towards this house, then fire.'

'I can do that. You know this is a muzzle-loader, though? It'll take me a minute or so to reload.'

'If you start shooting I'll be out here to join you. Don't fret about how long it's taking you to load.'

It was not the first time that Rick O'Shea had been south of the border and he was fairly familiar with the way of life in little villages such as this, where the chief defining feature was grinding poverty. The people living in this sort of place had no money to spare for shop-bought goods; they made pretty well all that they needed by the use of their own hands. This meant that doors were secured, if they were closed up, by simple wooden latches and the occasional bar. But nobody in a village such as Chuchuverical could be expected to own much that was worth stealing and it was ten to one against any of the doors even being barred from within.

So it proved, because a little gentle pressure caused the door to the white-painted adobe dwelling-house to open inwards at once. O'Shea slipped the pistol from its holster, cocking it with his thumb as he did so.

The house was pitch dark within and O'Shea wasn't minded to strike a lucifer to see what he was about. He hoped at all costs not to be compelled to shoot anybody, because he was sure that the sound of gunfire would invite enquiry at night. The windows were tiny and unglazed, with wooden shutters to close up in cold or windy weather. As his eyes adjusted to the dark he found that what scant moonlight filtered through into the interior of the little house was just about sufficient for his needs.

There was only one downstairs room and it contained nothing of interest. There was a clay oven, some bowls and vegetables, along with a few sticks of crude furniture: a table and two chairs. The sleeping-quarters must be upstairs. Very slowly, almost on tippy-toe, he made his way up the wooden ladder, which led to the upper storey.

There was more light up here and O'Shea could see at once that there were two beds in the single room. One was occupied by an old woman who was snoring stertorously, in the other lay a young girl. They were linked together by a length of rope, which connected their wrists. At the sight of this O'Shea's face hardened. He guessed that this old woman was probably kin to Yanez — was maybe even his mother — and that she was acting as guardian for the snatched child. Fancy tying the child to her by a rope, as though she were an animal!

Moving swiftly, O'Shea hopped up from the head of the ladder and entered the room. He woke the old woman by the simple expedient of jabbing her hard in the ribs with the barrel of his pistol. When he was sure that she was fully awake, he showed her the gun.

'I don't know how much English you understand,' he said quietly, 'but I can tell you now: if you make a noise I'll kill you. Understand?' The woman nodded and watched O'Shea fearfully. He had never in all his life harmed a woman and didn't mean to begin now, but there was no percentage in letting her know that. Keeping the gun pointing at her face, O'Shea gestured to her wrist.

'Undo it,' he said. Whether she understood his words or merely guessed what he wanted, he couldn't say, but she at once began to untie the rope that linked her to the sleeping child.

'That's the spirit,' he said, 'keep on like this and there's no need for anybody to get hurt.'

When the rope was free of the old woman's wrist O'Shea cast his eyes around the room and saw a few raggedy items of clothing scattered on the floor. He picked up something that might have been a scarf and proceeded to gag the woman. He did not tie the knot cruelly tight, but it was without doubt secure. Having done this, he went over to awaken the child who was slumbering in the other bed. He shook her shoulder gently and when her eyes opened he said softly:

'Don't be afeared, honey, your sister's waiting for you outside.'

'Oh, goody! Is it time for me to be going home now?'

'That's right. Just let me unfasten this piece of rope.'

'Oh, you mustn't do that,' she said in

alarm. 'They'll get cross with me if you do that.'

'Don't you worry about that, little one,' said O'Shea in a reassuring tone, as though he were talking to a much younger child. 'Nobody's going to get cross with you. I promise.'

Having taken the other end of the long piece of rope from the child's wrist he used it to bind the old Mexican woman hand and foot. Before he led little Emily down the ladder to, he hoped, safety, Rick O'Shea looked down into the old woman's eyes and delivered himself of the following sentiments:

'If you were a man I don't know but that I wouldn't have killed you for being involved in this business. Are you kin to Yanez?' He could see by the look in her eyes that she recognized the name. He concluded by saying:

'You be sure now to tell Yanez that if he and me ever meet, then I'll be calling him to account for this wickedness. And you, a woman, shame on you for having anything to do with it!' He shook his head in disgust, then shepherded the little girl down the ladder. When they were both at the bottom O'Shea pulled down the ladder, then wrenched it to pieces with his bare hands. This released some of his pent-up fury, which had been threatening to choke him.

Emily Covenay watched O'Shea nervously as he demolished the ladder and he felt a little ashamed of himself for scaring her.

'Come on, honey,' he said, 'let's get you reunited with that sister of yours. She's a rare one, I will say.'

Once O'Shea and Emily were outside the house the two sisters flew into each other's arms. The younger one began to prattle in a high, clear voice about her recent adventures.

'Hey, give over that,' said O'Shea in a hoarse whisper, 'we're not out of danger yet. We need to walk north to the river, right this very minute.'

Jemima explained in a low voice to

her sister that they had to keep quiet; then the little group began trudging towards the Rio Grande. Laughter could still be heard from Yanez's base, together with shouting and snatches of Spanish ballads. There seemed no present prospect of O'Shea's absence being noted, at least for some while yet and, with a little good fortune, for the whole night. If they could get across the river before daybreak it would give them a good start.

Once they were clear of Chuchuverical they let the excited child chatter a little, though hushing her when her voice rose too high or she began shouting with laughter. The little girl didn't seem to have had a bad time at all; apparently she regarded the whole episode as some sort of lark, the purpose of which was obscure to her.

O'Shea thought it a great mercy that she had no idea of the danger she had been in. He still could not believe that any man, no matter how depraved, could have undertaken a game of this sort. He shot a glance at the happy little creature skipping along by his side and was once again filled with a killing rage at the idea of anybody wishing to harm such a one.

His grim thoughts were interrupted by Jemima.

'You have yet to tell me your name, you know,' she said.

'To be sure: you're altogether right. I'm Rick O'Shea.'

'That your real name?'

'Of course. Why should I give a false one?'

Jemima chuckled. 'For Father Flaherty to have set you on this trail, I guess you must have made something of a confession. I never get more than saying ten Hail Marys.'

'You're sharp enough,' said O'Shea, smiling, 'but yes, that's really what I'm called.'

Emily, whose good spirits seemed to be irrepressible, piped up.

'It's such a lark to be up this late,' she

said. 'I'm never allowed to at home, am I, 'Mima?'

'You need your sleep,' her sister replied, looking at the child affectionately.

At O'Shea's insistence they all quietened down as they approached the Rio Grande. He had no idea of the procedure for crossing the great river at night. Surely, he who ran the ferry would be asleep at such an hour as this? The need was dire, though.

For all his assurances to the two girls that his escape would not be discovered until the next morning, O'Shea was very well aware that anybody might at any time notice that the roof of the shed in which he had been locked was now lying at an angle to the walls. That would be a mighty strong clue to anybody whose senses were not completely addled by liquor that something was amiss.

One thing was certain sure: it would not do for them to be caught on the wrong side of the river come first light.

Across the Rio Grande lights were twinkling in the town of Archangel. This was not a settlement of dirt farmers like Chuchuverical; few of those in Archangel needed to be up at dawn to wrest a living from the dusty and unproductive soil of these parts. There were in that little burg only those who, the Scriptures tell us, *toil not and neither do they spin*, along with a bunch of hotel-owners and saloon-keepers who catered for their needs. Sitting up all night drinking and gaming was what men did in Archangel and similar border towns. That being so, there was at least a chance that the ferryman would not yet be abed.

Their luck seemed to be in, because hanging from the landing stage used by the ferry on that side of the river was a massive brass bell which, by the look of it, had at one time been salvaged from some shipwreck. Although loath to advertise their presence in so noisy a manner, there was nothing else to be done, so O'Shea clanged the bell for all he was worth.

The old man was evidently not asleep, for he emerged from the log cabin in which he lived so as to be near his livelihood. He was carrying a storm lantern, which he held up high, and he called out across the water:

'What's to do? You want passage?'

'Yes, and as quick as you like,' shouted back O'Shea. 'Our need is pressing.'

'I'll be bound. Cost you a mort extra at this time o' night. You willin' to pay?'

'Yes. Just hurry it along.'

'Courtesy don't cost nothing. Wait up a minute.'

There was much creaking as the old man boarded his ferry, which was really little more than a raft, and began slowly and laboriously tugging on the rope, which would pull him to the opposite bank.

The ferry was just nearing the landing stage when Rick O'Shea heard a sound that told him his good fortune had just run out. It was the sound of hoof-beats, and it was coming from the direction of Chuchuverical. When he turned to look south he could see lights in or near the village: blazing pine knots, most likely.

Clearly, the alarm had been raised and an unknown number of men were now heading straight for him and the two girls. He turned to Jemima Covenay.

'If you're serious about getting your sister to safety, then now's the time to prove it,' he told her. 'You ready and willing to fire that gun of yours? At a man, that is.'

'If it's one of them as stole away my little sister, then it'll be my pleasure,' she replied coldly.

'Then take out one of those riders that's bearing down on us and be quick about it.'

Without more ado, and to O'Shea's enormous surprise, the girl crouched down. Resting her piece on a pile of logs she sighted down the barrel at the three horsemen who were galloping towards them and were now no more than a hundred yards away. It remained to be seen whether or not she would actually pull the trigger, but the fact that she had not cavilled at his order to shoot a man was at least encouraging.

O'Shea drew his pistol and cocked it; this proceeding caused the utmost alarm to the old man in charge of the ferry.

'What's this?' he cried out. 'I can't afford to be at outs with those boys from Chuchuverical.' He began to reverse direction, obviously prepared to abandon O'Shea and the Covenay sisters to the mercy of the bandits.

Turning towards the retreating ferryman, O'Shea drew down on him.

'You don't bring that heap o' lumber back here directly, I swear to God I'll kill you!' he shouted. There was a threatening urgency in Rick O'Shea's voice that warned the old man there was no percentage in crossing him. He began heaving on the rope again, bringing his little craft across to shore.

At that moment there was a loud crack from where Jemima Covenay had been crouching and one of the three riders fell from his horse; the animal went cantering off with the rider hanging by one ankle from a stirrup. O'Shea turned and fired twice at the other men, who reined in.

Then, not knowing how many armed adversaries they were facing, the men rode back the way they'd come. They pulled up a hundred yards off, waiting to see what the play was. O'Shea figured that this was the only chance he and the sisters would have and he called urgently to the older girl:

'Get your sister on board this very second.'

Young Emily was disposed to have a fit of the hysterics at the sudden outbreak of shooting, but Jemima Covenay quieted her as though she were a spooked steer and urged her on to the raft. O'Shea fired twice more in the general direction of the two riders, for all the good it might do at that range, then leaped aboard himself. The old man was fumbling with the rope so O'Shea elbowed him aside, taking over the task himself. Pulling as fast and as hard as he was able, he turned to the sisters.

'Lay yourselves down flat in case those villains start shooting at us,' he told them.

The words were no sooner out of his mouth than one of the men on the Mexican side drew a carbine from a scabbard hanging in front of his saddle and fired at the raft. It was a close shot: too close for comfort. The ball struck the water just six feet from the ferry, sending up a spray of water as it did so.

Knowing he had only one shot left, and considering the distance, O'Shea was almost in despair. He decided that his energy would be better used in getting the flimsy craft to the American side of the river, though how many of them would be alive by then, now that

that fellow had the range, was any-body's guess.

The boom of the next shot, practically at his elbow, came as a shock. Looking at the shore they had left O'Shea observed that another of the riders was down. It was apparently the one who had just fired at them. The surviving man did not appear anxious to wait there to be picked off; suddenly he spurred on his horse and galloped away towards Chuchuverical.

Rick O'Shea stopped hauling the rope and spoke to the ferryman.

'There you go, old man,' he said. 'You can take over now.' He turned to Jemima Covenay.

'You must have started reloading the second we came on board,' he said. 'I'll own to being impressed. You feeling all right after shooting those scoundrels?'

The young woman's eyes were as hard as pieces of glass.

'I told you before, I'd shoot any of them that did this,' she replied. 'You think I didn't mean it?'

The younger girl chipped in: 'What's this 'bout shooting, 'Mima? Who you gonna shoot?'

'Nobody at all, darling. Me and this here gentleman are just fooling around. There's nothing for you to fret about. Way past your bedtime. We need to get you a room for the night.'

There was unpleasantness when the ferry reached Archangel, for the old man demanded ten times the usual fare on account of he had been roused from his bed and had also had his very life set at hazard. O'Shea's only aim was to assist in getting Emily Covenay back to her home; he did not wish to throw around money that might be needed to pay for food and accommodation for the sisters, for whom he now felt responsible.

'See now, you can choose,' he said to the man. 'I'll give you five dollars or nothing. It's up to you, because you can see how I'm situated. It's life and death and I wouldn't think twice about gunning down anybody who gets crosswise to me. You understand me well enough, I see.'

In truth, the old man who operated the ferry understood with perfect clarity that over the next few days there would be good business for him; one result of the gun battle he had witnessed would be to draw a bunch of bandits seeking revenge from across the border.

'Well,' he said with an ill grace, 'let's see your money then.'

Once this had been attended to, Rick O'Shea was ready to consider what provision it would be best to make for the night, which was fast wearing away.

6

The main point under consideration, at least as far as Rick O'Shea was concerned, was whether or not a large band of Mexicans would cross the river that very night in search of both him and the child whom he and Jemima had taken. If so, he could hardly expect any help or support from anybody in Archangel. The inhabitants all had fish of their own to fry, and wouldn't thank him for bringing trouble down upon the town. For all he knew to the contrary, some of those here might even be friends of Yanez and his boys, inclined to take his part in any sort of dispute. At the very least nobody hereabouts would want trouble that might bring the law — or, God forbid, the military down on them.

All this necessitated coming to a decision as to whether O'Shea and the girls should try and find a room for the night there in town, or press on, making a run for San Angelo at once. The simple fact that he had only one horse, or just possibly two, made O'Shea decide that they would be well advised to stay in Archangel, at least until morning. He had his own mount, and according to Jemima Covenay she too had one, stabled in the same establishment as O'Shea's.

It might prove possible to persuade the fellow running the livery stable to part with Sheriff Jackson's mount as well but, when all was said and done, there were three of them to transport through the Reds. If it had been only himself and Jemima Covenay to consider it might have been possible to make a run for it, but he suspected that the little sister would not be up to galloping hell for leather through the Gap with a body of armed men on their tail. It certainly wouldn't work if one of the horses were carrying two people.

The most sensible dodge would be

to stay there that night and then, if the owner of the stable wouldn't part with Jackson's horse, try to get hold of some little pony the next day — assuming, of course, that Emily Covenay was actually able to ride. Otherwise, he supposed it might mean running across rough ground with a buggy or something of the kind.

'Can your sister ride?' he asked Jemima.

'Why don't you ask her? She's not a fool.' replied Jemima tartly.

'Sure I can ride,' affirmed Emily, catching the drift of their conversation. 'I can ride 'most as good as 'Mima. Ain't that right?'

'It is, darling. You're a most remark-able rider.'

'So, young Emily,' said O'Shea, 'if I could get hold of a pony or something, you reckon as you could ride for a couple of days?'

'Pony? I won't need no pony, will I, Jemima? I can ride big horses.'

'Well then,' said O'Shea, 'that might

make things a little easier. I dare say as somebody in this town'll be induced to sell us a horse.'

One of the hotels was still open for business — or at any rate the saloon on the ground floor was, and the manager was happy to rustle up a couple of poky little rooms. O'Shea's arrival in such a fashion with a couple of females, one of them only a child and the other dressed as a man, had attracted a good deal more attention than O'Shea would have wanted, but there was nothing to be done about it. The fact that the older of the females was carrying a military musket was also apt to make people talk after they'd left.

There was little doubt that if Yanez and his men or Seth Jackson showed up here, it wouldn't take too long for them to hear tidings of him and the Covenay sisters.

Before they turned in for the night O'Shea checked out the room that the two sisters would be sleeping in. He took the opportunity to reload the pistol that he had borrowed from Jemima. She had a neat little powder flask and full box of caps, along with a plentiful supply of balls and lint. As he charged the chambers of the gun, he said casually:

'And you ain't too distressed about that shooting earlier?'

For the first time since he had met her Jemima Covenay smiled: a radiant sight that warmed O'Shea's heart.

'It's real sweet of you to be worried about me,' she said, 'but really, I'm just fine. Those men should never have troubled my sister, then they wouldn't have got theyselves shot. I felt no more of it than if I'd shot a dog with the rabies.'

'You're the devil of a girl!' he exclaimed admiringly. 'I don't know when last I met somebody with as much grit as you got. I'll leave you two alone. Don't open that door for anybody but me. I'm in the next room; just bang on the wall if you've need. Goodnight, Emily. I hope you're looking forward to a good long ride tomorrow?'

'I can't wait. I love long rides.'

After giving some thought to staying awake all night and guarding the sisters next door, O'Shea came to the conclusion that he'd be fit for nothing the next day if he were to do so. He was a light sleeper and didn't doubt that he'd awaken if anything untoward happened.

As he lay on the bed, after having kicked off his boots, O'Shea suddenly realized that he had given no thought in the last twenty-four hours to the fact that he was not really a free agent in this mission. However, had he been released that very minute from the obligations laid upon him by the priest in San Angelo, he would still carry straight along on the same course. This was a comforting reflection: that his present inclinations coincided in all respects with his duty. It was, to say the very least of it, an uncommon state of affairs. With this thought Rick O'Shea fell sound asleep.

When next he opened his eyes daylight was flooding in through the window. The light had that pale and watery quality about it that you get just after dawn. O'Shea figured that it was no later than half-past five. He could only have been asleep for four or five hours, but that would have to do for now.

He pulled on his boots, opened the door and went out into the corridor. To his surprise Jemima answered him as soon as he called her name softly outside the door to her room.

'I'm awake and ready,' she said. 'Give Emily five minutes and we'll join you.'

O'Shea had the feeling that it was a shade under five minutes before the door to the sisters' room opened and they both came out. Emily was yawning sleepily, but Jemima Covenay looked as fresh as if she'd been on an especially relaxing vacation.

'I've to see about our horses for the journey to San Angelo,' said O'Shea. 'I shouldn't be gone more than a half-hour. We must move quickly. Can you both be ready to move by then? I've a notion they'll serve you coffee down in the saloon if you ask.'

'We'll be ready,' said Jemima Covenay.

The fellow in charge of the livery stable was amenable to the idea of O'Shea taking both his own and Sheriff Jackson's horse, providing always that both bills were settled. It was while he was on his way back to the hotel that Rick O'Shea caught sight of Seth Jackson, striding down the street as large as life.

It shouldn't really have been any great surprise to see the sheriff here. After Rick O'Shea's escape from captivity it would have taken no great exercise of intellect to work out that he would be heading across the border. The discovery, which must surely have been made by now, that the child was also free, must have made this conclusion a racing certainty. Well then, O'Shea was not about to let Jackson spoil his game; not by a long sight.

Sheriff Jackson was walking briskly past the space between a hardware store and one of Archangel's less salubrious saloons when he received an almighty shove from behind, which almost sent him sprawling into the dirt. Before he had recovered his balance somebody had grabbed hold of him and hustled him into the alleyway between the two buildings. The whole action had taken only a few seconds.

Either nobody had noticed what had chanced or those who frequented the main street of Archangel were in the habit of minding their own business and not getting mixed up in things that were no concern of theirs. Whatever the reason, nobody appeared to take any notice of the scuffle. As soon as the two men were out of view of anyone in the street Rick O'Shea cocked his piece and thrust the barrel of the .36 pistol painfully up into Sheriff Jackson's throat, right at the angle of his jaw. He did this while still gripping Jackson's arm, it being made clear in this way to the sheriff that if there were to be any struggling or fighting he was likely to have his head blown off. Despite this rough handling, Jackson said in a civil enough voice:

'What'll you have, O'Shea? You know it's a hanging matter if you go any further down this road?'

'I just want the favour of a word, is all. First off is where others in this here town know now about your villainy. Disposing of me won't save you and word about it is already like to be on its way to San Angelo.'

This was a bold bluff, but O'Shea figured that it might put the wind up Jackson, who merely asked, still in a conversational tone of voice:

'Anything more?'

'Just this. I got no interest in chasing after crooked lawmen right now, nor killing of them either. You leave me be and I'm going to return that poor child to her folks. You try and hinder me, and before God I'll lay you in your grave and be hanged to the consequences of it.'

Surprisingly, Jackson laughed at this.

'You won't make it back to San Angelo,' he said, 'not after what you done, O'Shea.'

'What *I* done? What's that mean? Speak up now.'

'You killed Yanez's mother and his baby brother last night. When I left last night he was swearing oaths by all the gods that he was going to torture you to death.'

'His mother? What're you talking about?'

'Well,' said Jackson, chuckling as though he was at a musical theatre or some other light entertainment, 'it was you, I guess, as hog-tied the old woman and gagged her? She tumbled down after you carried out your rescue last night. Fell down from her bedroom and broke her neck in the dark. You take the ladder away, too?'

He saw from the look in O'Shea's face that his question needed no other reply; he smiled again.

'Well then, you're a woman killer. How's that make you feel? Still feel you're a better man than me?'

For Rick O'Shea, who had always prided himself on not harming a single hair on the head of any woman or child, it was the hell of a shock, although he was not about to let Sheriff Jackson see that. He didn't speak for a second; he and Jackson just stood there in their awkward poses, as though they were part of a waxwork tableau. Then O'Shea spoke.

'I'm sorry that the old woman died and I own freely that I am answerable for her death. Even so, I reckon her blood is upon her own head. Anybody becomes mixed up in such a filthy business as that, man or woman, they got to abide by the results of it. She'd tied a rope round that poor child's arm, like she was a dog or steer.

'I'll answer for her death to Yanez, maybe, but I'd do the same thing again if it brought that little girl to safety.'

'Why, you are one cold-hearted bastard,' said Sheriff Jackson wonderingly. 'Wait 'til Yanez catches up with you.'

'I suppose one of them I shot last night was his brother? Well, I'll answer for that too, though I don't feel a bit sorry. This ain't business, Jackson. You might be a lawman, but I reckon you'll have your work cut out rustling up any posse or finding citizens to assist you in any way in a town like this.

'Tell you what I'll do. I'll turn you loose, but on the understanding that you keep clear of me. Were I you, I wouldn't go back to San Angelo, for they'll soon know what a wretch you are there.'

'I don't believe you've had time to send word anywhere. You're bluffing.'

'Well, I ain't bluffing about this: I catch a sight of you afore I leave this town, I'm like to kill you. That's no bluff.'

O'Shea took his gun from Jackson's neck and released his arm, but he still kept the pistol pointing vaguely in the sheriff's direction.

'Go on, get out of here,' he said.

As he made his way back to the hotel O'Shea thought to himself, *I reckon that with good fortune and a fair wind behind me, I have no more than ten minutes to collect those horses and get out of here. Jackson's a snake and he won't forgive being held so at gunpoint.*

The two girls had had a bite to eat and O'Shea hurried them out of the hotel and down to the livery stable and yard. It was at this point that things miscarried, because O'Shea had been fixing to take Sheriff Jackson's horse for Emily but, even though they had come straight here within a matter of ten or fifteen minutes of his parting company with Jackson, the sheriff had still had time to collect his horse.

'How long since he collected his mount?' asked O'Shea of the man running the livery stable. 'Can't have been that long since.'

'You the law?' enquired the man pertinently. 'No? Thought not. Just worry about paying your own bill, never mind cross-questioning me about other folk's business. We don't care over much round here for those as ask a heap o' questions.'

'We need to buy a horse. Tack, too,' said O'Shea after a moment's thought. 'Can you help?'

'That's more like it,' replied the man, brightening considerably. 'This *is* business. Come round back; I got the very thing.'

The man's idea of 'the very thing' turned out to be a scrawny-looking beast that looked as though it was on its last legs. To hear the stableman talk, though, you'd have thought that the nag was on a par with the legendary Pegasus.

O'Shea interrupted the man's spiel to settle on a firm price, which was, all things considered, less than he had feared. Beggars, however, cannot be choosers, so O'Shea took the horse and paid about twice what it was worth. He could, he supposed, always sell it on when he got back to San Angelo. The saddle and bridle smelled of mildew and looked to Rick O'Shea's eye like they'd been mouldering away in some hayloft since the Devil was a boy.

Time was pressing, so he paid cash down for both horse and tack. Within another ten minutes they were on their way north, heading towards the Reds.

It was pleasing to O'Shea to observe that the elder of the two sisters had not once asked anything about the dealings he'd engaged in while buying the horse. She might be a tough one, but she had been well brought up. Nevertheless, from time to time he caught her looking sideways at him, as though waiting for him to offer some explanation of the transaction she had witnessed. It was only right that she should know something of how matters stood, he supposed.

'You don't mind I call you just Jemima?' asked O'Shea, once they were on the road. 'We've no time for fancy manners.'

'Go ahead. You've some urgent news, I can see. Let's be having it.'

'The fellow that took your little sister might be coming after us. He's not after her, but me.'

'Why?'

'That's nothing to the purpose. The point is, you might have to take your sister home without my help. Reckon you can manage that?'

Emily Covenay piped up at this point.

'We going home now, 'Mima? I'm surely glad,' she said excitedly.

'Yes, we're going home, darling. This gentleman is just working out some details with me. Nothing for you to fret about. Just enjoy the ride.' Jemima Covenay turned back to O'Shea. 'You're wrong, you know. We're all in this together. You think anybody'll want a living witness to this? You know it's me and Emily as well as you in the frame.'

140

Not for the first time, Rick O'Shea was struck by the coolness of the young woman in the face of danger.

'Let's see what comes, then,' he replied. 'I only wanted you to know that I'll do whatever's needed to get your little sister home. I won't abandon you.'

'I already knew that,' replied Jemima.

O'Shea ran over in his mind the probable course of events. There could be no doubt that Jackson would team up with Yanez when he crossed the Rio and landed in Archangel. What then? Would the sheriff try to guy up his pursuit as some kind of lawful enterprise? Might he even deputize Yanez's band of cut-throats and make out that they were a legitimate posse? That would perhaps solve everybody's problems. Yanez would be able to kill O'Shea and then Jackson and the others would murder the Covenay sisters, pretending that they had got caught in the crossfire.

He, Rick O'Shea, would be denounced as the man who had stolen away the child in the first place and then those bastards would even be able to collect on the reward being offered and divide it up between themselves. Following which, Seth Jackson would be re-elected sheriff of the county once more.

Well, they wouldn't get away with it; not while Rick O'Shea had breath in his body they wouldn't.

Jemima Covenay interrupted O'Shea's reverie with a question.

'We heading for the Gap? That's the only way through the Reds, ain't it? Leastways, it's how I got to Archangel.'

'Well, it is and it isn't,' replied O'Shea thoughtfully. 'Truth to tell, I'm not overly keen on us riding along on flat land such as this and just waiting for anybody to come after us; you understand what I'm saying?'

'Of course I do,' said the young woman, casting an anxious glance at her sister in order to reassure herself that the child wasn't getting alarmed by all this talk of people pursuing them. 'What then d'ye suggest? We're altogether in your hands, for I don't know this part of the county at all.'

'I heard tell that there's a path leading up and over the Reds, a mule trail or something of the kind.'

'A mule trail? Why would you need such a thing? That gap's been there time out of mind, from what I gather.'

'There's been silver-mining up in the Reds. Lead as well. There's an ore that the English call 'galena', which is lead mixed with silver. Grey, shiny stuff. Anyways, I heard that there's old mine workings up there. Maybe anybody riding the same path as us would miss us if they didn't know which road we'd taken.'

The mountains loomed up in the distance. O'Shea wondered whether they would be able to reach them before those seeking his blood caught up with them and killed them all.

'We need to ride hard for the Reds,' he said. 'Young Emily, can you gallop that horse, do you think?'

''Course I can gallop,' she cried

indignantly. 'Tell him how well I can gallop, 'Mima.'

'Well, I'm sorry to cause offence,' said O'Shea hastily. 'Let's make for those mountains then.'

It was a fine calculation to make: forcing as hard a pace as possible but without exhausting their beasts or, worse still, laming one of the mounts. Still, the three of them made it to the foothills at the base of the Reds by noon and there was still no sign of anybody coming after them.

It was a matter then of finding the path which supposedly led up into the mountains. This proved surprisingly easy and Rick O'Shea was feeling right pleased with himself as they made their way up the serpentine track that wound its way up the rocky slopes towards the ridge, which was about three thousand feet above them. That was, until events took an unexpected turn, causing both Jemima Covenay and Rick O'Shea to wonder whether maybe the child they had rescued wasn't perhaps destined to die prematurely anyway, despite their efforts.

This is what happened.

The three of them were proceeding in single file as their horses plodded along the stony trail. Emily had begged to lead the way and neither O'Shea nor Jemima could see any reason to deny the child her wish. To their left were slopes which led down to the gap, where the railroad lines gleamed in the midday sun; to the right was the vast mass of the mountains across which they hoped to make their way. Suddenly, unexpectedly Emily reined in.

'Look, 'Mima,' she cried in an excited voice, 'there's a locomotive coming along.'

So abruptly had Emily Covenay halted that the other two riders almost collided into each other. At that same moment a shot rang out, causing Emily's horse to rear up and send her crashing to the ground. There she lay, apparently lifeless.

7

Where shooting was concerned Rick O'Shea had an uncanny ability to calculate, just from the sound, where the firing was from and at what distance. He also had a shrewd idea, from hearing a single shot, whether the weapon being discharged was a pistol, rifle or scattergun.

In this instance he judged that somebody had fired with a carbine at distance of, perhaps, a hundred yards to their left, which was to say: in the direction of Grey John's Gap. Before the echo had died down O'Shea was off his horse and had dragged Jemima Covenay from hers. The young woman struggled to get up from the ground.

'I got to get to Emily, she said. 'There's blood on her head.'

'It won't help her none if you get killed,' said O'Shea harshly. 'Lie still here, by these rocks. Whoever fired at us is lower down. We can't be seen from down there. We must a' been silhouetted up against the sky, which is what gave him his target.'

His cool and collected manner worked to some purpose, for Jemima Covenany stopped fighting him and said quietly:

'I'm going to wriggle across to my sister. I'll keep low.'

While the young woman crawled over on her belly to see to the injured child, Rick O'Shea cursed himself for a damned fool who had brought these poor sisters into deadly hazard. He really should have known better and, without even thinking the matter through consciously, he knew now just exactly what had occurred.

So busy had O'Shea been with setting a watch to make sure that they weren't being followed by Yanez and his gang that he had hardly given a thought to the one or two riders he could see ahead of him. He had been so damned certain-sure that Seth Jackson would be making common cause with Yanez that he hadn't paused for a moment to consider that the sheriff might have his own motives for silencing O'Shea and doing away with Emily and her sister.

It wasn't a matter of missing out on a reward or failing to be voted in as sheriff in a few weeks. If O'Shea told all he knew, then Jackson would stand an excellent chance of being lynched by the men of San Angelo.

All this went through O'Shea's mind before Jemima Covenay had reached her sister. When she got to Emily she found that the blood was just from a slight cut on her head, where she had fallen from her horse and banged her forehead against a rock. The little girl had been stunned, but was now coming round and beginning to sob.

'Jemima,' O'Shea said, 'is that musket of yours primed and charged?'

'Yes,' she answered distractedly, 'but it's on my horse yonder.'

When he looked up it was to discover

that Jemima's horse had trotted on ahead and was now in a position where anybody approaching it would be in plain view from the slope below. He'd have to make do with the pistol, which was a nuisance. He risked a quick glance over the rocks that were sheltering them from view and nearly had his head shot off as a result. Sheriff Jackson was positioned less than a hundred yards away, with his rifle resting on a boulder, the better to judge his aim.

The only good thing about their current situation was the reflection that had they simply ridden through the Gap they'd all be dead by now. It was plain as a pikestaff that Jackson had counted on their riding hard through Grey John's Gap in their haste to get back to San Angelo. He'd found a nice vantage point overlooking the Gap and all he had needed to do was wait until they passed below and then pick them off one by one; including, thought O'Shea in mounting fury, a little girl who wasn't in full possession of her wits. It was the most devilish scheme he'd ever heard tell of in the whole course of his life.

There was nothing for it but that he would have to act immediately, thought O'Shea to himself. At any moment Yanez might come riding out from Archangel and then it would be all up with them. He had to deal with Jackson without any delay. He called over to the elder sister.

'Come over here, Jemima. Leave your sister for a moment and attend to me. It's life and death for us all.'

After murmuring some reassuring words to Emily the older girl scurried across to where Rick O'Shea lay prone.

'What are we going to do?' she asked.

'What I'm going to do is run down that slope and kill the man down there. While I'm doing that you must run to your horse and fetch out that rifle of yours. I'll keep that devil too busy to trouble you while you do it. Then, if anything happens to me, you must be sure that you're ready to kill him before he knows what's what.'

'It's certain death for you to go after him that way. Is there nothing else?'

'I'm no keener on dying than you, Jemima, but 'less you got another plan, I reckon as we'll go with mine.' There was the ghost of smile round his lips as he said this; suddenly the girl leaned forward and kissed him on the cheek.

'Good luck,' she said, her voice choked.

'Just be ready to move as soon as I jump up,' said O'Shea.

Then, because he had already wasted enough time explaining his intentions, and with Yanez perhaps already on the road from Archangel, Rick O'Shea drew the gun from its holster, leaned over the rocks and snapped off a single shot at Seth Jackson. Then he leaped up and ran at full speed towards the startled sheriff.

There was not, despite the apparent recklessness of his action, any intention on Rick O'Shea's part to throw away his life. He knew that firing at a stationary target is a very different thing indeed from shooting at somebody moving rapidly and erratically, so as he ran he jinked from side to side, making it impossible for the man on the slope below to guess where he would be in the next second. He also fired twice as he was running, not because he thought he could hit Jackson with his pistol while running in this way, but simply to spoil the other fellow's aim and prevent him from settling down to take careful aim.

Several shots came close and O'Shea wondered if he would be able to get the sheriff to expend enough ammunition to make it necessary for him to reload. He must have fired four times now. O'Shea sent another wild shot in Jackson's direction, just as the other man fired.

At that moment he twisted his ankle as he stumbled on a loose rock. O'Shea found himself tumbling forward, landing behind a boulder. There came another shot. It hit the boulder behind which O'Shea was sheltering and sent chips of rock flying off. Then there was silence and he wondered if Jackson might think that he had taken him down. In the heat of battle a man flying forward in the way that he had done might have looked like a direct hit.

He looked up to the trail where he had left the Covenay sisters and was pleased to observe that only the horses were visible. It was to be doubted that Jackson would think it worth expending any ammunition on their mounts, which gave O'Shea reason to hope that they might yet make it back to San Angelo.

Then there came a puff of smoke from up on the trail and, a fraction of a second later, the boom of Jemima Covenay's rifle. This was followed by a perfect fusillade of shots from Jackson, which ended abruptly. It was now or never. O'Shea rose to his feet, cocking the pistol with his thumb as he did so. Twenty yards away Sheriff Jackson was fumbling frantically with the carbine in his hands.

'Over here, Jackson,' O'Shea called out.

Seth Jackson looked up fearfully. Before he had a chance to duck or take any other evasive action O'Shea drew down on him and fired twice. Both balls struck the sheriff in his chest. Taking no chances, O'Shea sprinted to where Jackson stood looking down stupidly at the two holes that indicated his worthless life had run its course and was fast drawing to a close. Rick O'Shea grabbed the rifle from Jackson's hands and gave him a kick, sending him to the ground. From overhead came Jemima Covenay's voice, calling:

'Are you all right? I thought he'd taken you.'

'Not a bit of it,' O'Shea shouted back cheerfully. 'God takes care of fools sometimes. I'm fine. How's that sister of yours?'

'Shaken up and bruised, but she'll do.'

It took only a couple of minutes to loot Sheriff Jackson's corpse — and pretty lean pickings there were to be had, too. The only items of any value or use were the dead man's rifle, a Winchester '73, and his pistol. There were plenty of shining brass shells for both weapons but only five dollars in cash money. The sheriff's crooked life did not seem to have made him all that wealthy.

Once O'Shea had regained the trail he cast an anxious glance back in the direction of Archangel. He saw, to his relief but not inconsiderable surprise, that there was no sign yet of any body of riders heading north.

'We might make it yet. We might just,' he muttered to himself.

Emily's good spirits did not seem noticeably dented by her having been shot at, fallen from her horse and stunned, followed in quick order by being caught up in a gun battle. As they remounted a broad grin split the child's face.

'Gosh!' she said. 'That was an awful

noise all them guns made. I put my hands right over my ears, didn't I, 'Mima?'

'You did just fine, darling.'

'I'll sure be glad to get home. Won't Pa be surprised when he hears the larks we've been up to? You bet he'll laugh his head off.'

Jemima Covenay's eyes met O'Shea's and, hearing this innocent expectation from the excited child, they both smiled.

'I'm not sure that he'll laugh all that much, Miss Emily,' O'Shea said, 'but let's get you home anyways.'

'I'm sorry I missed my shot,' said Jemima a little abruptly. 'I guess I'm not used to shooting at targets that are firing back.'

'It takes a bit of getting used to, I'll allow,' replied O'Shea. 'But it was having him distracted by your firing on him that gave me my chance.'

'Why did you shout out to him and alert him to your whereabouts afore you shot him?'

Rick O'Shea looked a little embarrassed at the question and rubbed his chin before answering.

'Why, the truth of the matter,' he said at last, 'is that if anybody was going to get killed I'd sooner it was me than you, I suppose. Had he drilled me, then it might o' given you the time to reload and finish him off.'

This was something of a conversation stopper, so the three of them mounted up and set off without speaking again.

Fortunately the winding track soon led them into the space between two of the peaks and out of view both of the plain that lay between the Reds and Archangel, and of Grey John's Gap. If Yanez was coming after them there was every chance that he'd ride straight through the Gap and so miss them entirely.

The worst that could be said of that journey across the Reds was that it was tedious. There was little to be seen other than bare rock, scrappy brown grass and the occasional clump of bristlecone pines. Their path led them to some abandoned mine workings, which occupied much of a little plateau and prompted O'Shea to suggest that they could do worse than spend the night there. As he reasoned the case out to the elder sister:

'We're not going to hit San Angelo today and I don't altogether feel easy about sleeping out in the open.'

It was plain that young Emily didn't take to this scheme, having had more than enough adventures by this time and wanting only to be tucked up safe and sound in her soft bed at home, but her sister could see the sense in what O'Shea was saying and sided with him on the point.

'We won't have to sleep in that dark cave, will we?' the little girl asked nervously. 'I'm scared of it. Anything could live there.'

'Don't you worry none,' O'Shea told her. 'We'll just sleep out under the stars. You never done that before? It's rare fun, I tell you. Be something else for you to tell your father about when you get home.'

At this the child brightened up and was soon chattering away to her sister about how much she would have to tell their pa when their adventure was over.

'Mind, I shouldn't wonder if he don't take his buggy-whip to me when we do get home,' Jemima remarked to O'Shea. 'I came down here without asking so much as a by-your-leave.'

'I'll talk to him, set things out straight. Had you not come I doubt I'd have managed this. It's took all that the two of us could manage to get this far.'

It might have been thought that following her kidnap, rescue, fall from the horse and having been in close proximity to a duel in which one man was killed, Emily Covenay had used up all her chances lately, but she was to face another mortal hazard before the little party set off the next day.

There was little enough to eat and drink; only the meagre provisions that remained in Jemima Covenay's pack, and by common consent they allotted the lion's share to Emily. She was ravenously hungry after all the riding that day. While stuffing bits of dry bread and more-or-less stale cheese into her mouth she talked about the day's events.

'I never rode so long in one day. I'm awful tired now, though. Can we sleep soon, 'Mima? You think we might be home tomorrow? I hope so. It's been fun, but I miss Pa.'

She turned to address O'Shea directly. 'I was sorry you tied up that old lady, you know,' she remarked. 'You think somebody would have come by and untied her by now? She was all right. A bit of a crosspatch, but kind of sweet too, if you know what I mean.'

'Emily, darling,' said her sister, 'don't speak while you're eating. It's not at all ladylike.'

'Sorry. I didn't think that manners mattered out here. What do you think?' She turned again to O'Shea.

'I don't know that I'm the best man to consult on manners and such,' said O'Shea with a laugh. 'I ain't moved in those circles where fancy behaviour was needed. But you'd best mind your sister, if nothing else.'

All three of them were dog-tired and they settled down to sleep as best they could, even before it was completely dark. Emily took quite a bit of settling and her sister fussed around her, trying to make the child as comfortable as could be in the circumstances. For his own part, O'Shea fell asleep almost at once and slumbered soundly until dawn, when he was awoken by a ferocious roaring sound, accompanied by frantic screaming.

Emily Covenay had had a restless night's sleep, tossing and turning on the stony soil where she lay. When she finally drifted off at around midnight, it was to doze fitfully, her sleep disturbed by lurid and alarming nightmares in which she was chased through dark passages by unknown but terrifying creatures.

At first light she opened her eyes and was enchanted to see what appeared to be an animated toy snuffling around a few feet away from her head. It was something big and black and furry and Emily felt an overwhelming desire to throw her arms around whatever it was and cuddle it. She accordingly threw off the rough blanket which her sister had placed tenderly over her sleeping form and stood up. The furry creature did not seem at all nervous of her, but evinced what Emily took to be the desire to play. It gambolled around a little in front of her, then scuttled off a few yards and turned round to peer back at her, for all the world as though it wanted to say: 'Come and catch me!' Nothing loath, she scooted across to the little ball of fur and attempted to throw her arms around it.

Having lived the whole of her life on a farm, which she left only to visit a town, it was not to be expected that Emily Covenay would be familiar with the ways of black bears. She had from time to time glimpsed them from a distance, but had never been this close to one, let alone one like this, which was so playful. The cub was only three months old and, although it weighed a good thirty pounds, was very much still a baby.

Black bear cubs are especially vulnerable to predators and it is common for them to be carried off by bobcats, wolves and mountain lions. For this reason, their mothers tend to be acutely sensitive to any perceived threat to the young and although black bears are in the usual way of things fairly timid and shy of humans, a mother with cubs can represent a great danger to those who are foolish enough to come to close.

So it was in this case, because as Emily Covenay chased the cub and it ran from her, an enormous female bear emerged from the mouth of the old mine and, after giving a tremendous roar, lumbered straight after what she believed to be a mortal hazard to her offspring.

Even first thing in the morning, as it was now, Rick O'Shea's mind worked out matters relating to life and danger of death very quickly and efficiently. He saw that a gigantic bear was reared up on its hind legs, roaring and trying to get at something which was cowering behind an old wooden cart. Then he glimpsed a smaller shape, which he saw at once could only be a bear cub.

Everything fell into place at once and he knew that the most urgent priority was to get that bear away from its intended target. Already it was pushing its bulk against the wagon, heaving it aside to get at the terrified child wedged behind it. The obvious way to distract the bear from its prey was to offer it a new diversion for its wrath, so O'Shea jumped up and ran over to the cub, making roaring noises of his own as though he meant to eat up the little ball of black fur.

Rick O'Shea's gambit worked better

than he could possibly have hoped, for the she-bear instantly forgot whatever lay behind that old cart and turned its attention to a new threat to the cub. For a creature of such great bulk, it moved faster than you would think possible and began running towards O'Shea, with the evident intention of tearing him to pieces.

For short bursts, a black bear can run almost as fast as a racehorse and O'Shea had no time to plan anything. All he could hope to do was remain out of reach of those teeth and claws. He ducked behind a boulder, just in time to avoid a mighty swipe from a paw which was almost the size of his head. Then there sounded a *crack*. The bear let out another roar of anger and turned away from him. Jemima Covenay had snatched up the pistol that he had taken from Jackson after their little contretemps and she had fired at the bear, seemingly hitting it. The sight of that slim woman, dressed in boy's clothes and with her hair cut short, standing there facing down a bear with the pistol in her hand, left a memory that stayed with Rick O'Shea for the rest of his life.

Infuriated by the pain of the ball, which it received in its side, the bear bounded across the clearing towards Jemima, who fired twice more before the beast skidded to a halt and collapsed only a dozen feet from the white-faced young woman. O'Shea hurried over to her.

'I never saw the like in my life,' he said. 'There's not one man in a thousand would've stood his ground like that, with the animal charging at you and all.'

'It's not the first bear I killed. Though the last occasion was with a rifle. I didn't know if this pistol would answer or not.'

'Yet you stood your ground still,' said O'Shea, admiringly. 'You never flinched.'

'I have to tend to my sister. Excuse me.'

O'Shea quite expected young Emily to develop a fit of hysteria and he, for one, would not have blamed her in the slightest. Truth to tell, he felt a little shaken himself by the onslaught of the bear. But Emily, whatever shortcomings she might have mentally, showed the same tough resilience that he so admired in her big sister. She seemed quite stoical about the whole business when once her sister had explained that the mother bear was only looking out for her cub.

'Like you look after me, you mean, 'Mima?'

'Just so, darling. You know how cross I'd be if anybody hurt you? That's all that mother bear was about. She didn't know that you were just playing with her cub, see.'

'Just a mistake, you mean?'

'That's right, just a mistake.'

O'Shea spoke up.

'Tell me, how'd you know where to shoot the thing? I've heard tell of men emptying their guns at a bear and the thing still carrying on and mauling 'em.'

'When you're hunting big animals, you have to aim for the dead centre of their brain,' the girl explained. 'That's what my pa taught me. Imagine a line running from ear to ear, and wherever you're firing from, you have to aim for the mid-point on that line. So when that bear came for me, I knew I had to shoot right between its eyes if I was to kill it.'

'You gave me to understand that you was no great shakes with pistols,' remarked O'Shea. 'That don't square up with what I saw this day.'

'I'm better with a rifle.'

After all the noise and shooting, Rick O'Shea deemed it wise for them to be leaving the vicinity sooner rather than later. The horses were looking a little droopy and could do with some water and feed. The three animals had remained surprisingly untroubled by the bear's antics and the subsequent shooting.

'One thing which is encouraging,' O'Shea said to Jemima, out of earshot of her sister, 'is that Yanez has either given up on hunting me down or he took the road through the Gap, as I hoped. Either way, he didn't come upon us while we were sleeping and cut our throats, which is something to be thankful for, at any rate.'

'Yes,' said Jemima drily. 'We must thank heaven for small mercies.'

By the time they were ready to move out the bear cub appeared to realize that its mother was no longer around to protect it. The little thing was nuzzling its mother's lifeless body and making pitiful mewing noises, which put them in mind of a lost kitten.

'It's awful sad,' Emily said. 'Can we take the baby bear along of us?'

'No,' said O'Shea, in a voice which brooked no opposition, 'we most certainly cannot.'

8

They were all of them getting hungry by the time the sun was fairly up in the sky, although where they were likely to obtain food and drink between there and San Angelo was something of a mystery, at least to Rick O'Shea. As they picked their way over the ridge and down to the level ground on the other side of the Reds they chanced upon a sparkling mountain stream, which meant that the three travellers and their mounts were at least able to slake their thirst.

'There looked from up there to be something in the way of a farm or smallholding over to our right,' O'Shea said when they had all drunk their fill. 'It might not take us far from our path were we to ride over and enquire if they'd be kind enough to sell us some bread or something.'

'I'm hungry,' said Emily, 'real hungry. Can we go and get some food, 'Mima?'

'If Mr O'Shea thinks it a good idea, then I don't see why not.'

The three of them trotted in the general direction of the little house in the fields that O'Shea had spotted from the mountainside. It lay only a little way off the track that led to the Gap. As they neared the place the hairs on the back of Rick O'Shea's neck had risen and were tickling him.

'Rein in, the pair of you,' he said.

'What is it?' asked Jemima, looking around to see if O'Shea had spotted something that she had missed.

'I couldn't rightly say,' replied O'Shea slowly, 'but something's amiss. Take my word for it.'

They were only a half-mile or so from the neat little house, which looked as innocent and inviting a building as you could hope to find.

'You two wait here,' O'Shea said. 'Don't come on at all unless I give you the word to do so.' Then he spurred on his mare, drawing the pistol from its holster and cocking it as he went.

When he'd reached the rail fence surrounding the farmhouse O'Shea called out in a loud voice:

'Hallo, in there! Anybody at home?' There was no reply. He noticed that the door was slightly ajar.

How he knew that there was death around, Rick O'Shea would have been quite unable to say. Perhaps he picked up subliminally on clues that his conscious mind did not notice and built up a picture in that way, or maybe it really was a sixth sense for danger: something quite inexplicable. Whatever it was, he knew before he'd even dismounted that he was about to see something unpleasant.

He was proved right when he kicked open the door of the little farmhouse and found a man and woman lying on the floor surrounded by more blood than O'Shea had ever seen in his life before. The two people, presumably the owners of this place, had both been slaughtered like hogs, by having their throats cut.

Although by no means a squeamish man, even O'Shea was slightly sickened by what he saw. In spite of this, his revulsion did not prevent him from making his way to the kitchen and seeing what vittles, if any, were to be found there. There was nothing to be done for those poor devils and his chief — indeed only — concern at that moment was getting that poor child safely back to her home.

There was a burlap sack lying in one corner of the kitchen, which O'Shea filled with all the eatables upon which he could lay his hands. There was bread, apples, cheese and a haunch of ham, together with a few oatcakes. Enough perhaps to keep three people going until sundown. Then, treading carefully around the corpses, around which a cloud of flies was buzzing, he left the house and saddled up.

Judging by the fact that the blood was only just congealing around the very edges of the pools, O'Shea figured that those people had died only a few hours earlier.

When he rode back to where the Covenay sisters were waiting for him patiently, O'Shea forced his face into a smile. This was enough to deceive Emily, but not her elder sister.

'What's to do?' she asked.

'I'll tell you later. We need to get away from here as soon as might be.'

'Which way? Straight for San Angelo?'

'I don't know and that's the honest to God's truth of it. Which side of town does your father's spread lie on?'

'You mean, do we come to it before reaching town?' queried Jemima. 'No, we live about four miles past the town from here. Why?'

'Because I'm afeared that we've got somebody holding the road against us and I'm thinking on what's best.'

Emily was talking quietly to her horse, so O'Shea walked his mount closer to Jemima and lowered his voice.

'To speak plainly,' he said, 'there's two dead people in that house yonder. One of them is a woman.'

'You think it's Yanez and his men?'

'It'd be the hell of a coincidence were there to be two bands of murderous rogues on the loose in the district. No, I reckon it was him.'

In the end there didn't seem to be any other choice than to head straight for San Angelo and then perhaps to skirt around the town, either to the east or to the west. Even that was a doubtful and debatable point. Would they be safer in the town itself? Yanez obviously knew where the Covenays lived. Might he not fetch up there and wait in ambush?

In the usual way of things O'Shea would have a pretty good idea of what to do: whether to fight or to cut and run, for example. Now, his hands were tied and it was not a pleasing state of affairs. He could not just ride off and leave these girls to fend for their own selves. He had to work out what was best for others besides himself.

They were all hungry, so they dismounted and had breakfast. O'Shea marvelled anew at the astonishing resilience shown by Emily Covenay. Her recent encounter with an angry bear, bent on killing her, did not appear to have dented her good spirits in the least, and she talked cheerfully while they ate. Jemima was a little more sober, wondering, like O'Shea, if they were likely to get back safely. When they had finished eating and had washed down the cheese and ham with draughts of water from the canteens, O'Shea spoke to Emily.

'I hope you won't take it amiss,' he said, 'if I have a private word with your sister, Emily. It's just about our route, you understand.'

'Don't mind me. 'Mima, can I have some more cheese?'

'Just a little, darling. You don't want to make yourself sick, you know.'

The two adults walked a little distance from the child.

'I reckon as we're best heading to San Angelo, rather than going to your father's place first,' O'Shea said when they were out of earshot.

'How so?'

'Yanez is after killing me, that's certain. I reckon as he's likely given up hope of getting any reward. It's just what the Italians call a vendetta now. You mind what I mean?'

'I heard of such things,' said Jemima. 'But, without meaning to be rude, how does that affect me and my sister?'

'Your sister knows a heap. Yanez, like as not, don't know about her . . . infirmity. For all he knows to the contrary, she could testify — get him hanged — if he was caught the wrong side of the border one day. He'd sleep easier if she were dead. Then again, I wouldn't want you and Emily to get caught up in any crossfire. There's liable to be sparks flying when me and Yanez cross paths. I was thinking, what about that old priest — Father Flaherty, is it?'

'You think Father Flaherty'd be some

help to you in a shoot-out?'

Despite the grimness of their predicament, O'Shea smiled and so did Jemima.

'You surely got grit, Jemima, to be joshing at such a time as this,' he said. 'No, I was wondering if we could leave Emily in his care? I don't look for Yanez to start a gun battle on Main Street. We might ride into San Angelo, then I could leave you and your sister with the good father and let what will come, come.'

'I'll thank you not to talk of 'leaving me' anywhere, like I was a parcel or a lost umbrella,' said the young woman with some asperity. 'I've a crow of my own to pluck with that bandit for what he's done.'

'No! Don't even think of it. I'll set to with Yanez if need be. You have no part of it.'

'Well, let's do as you say and take Emily to safety. We can talk more then.'

The journey to San Angelo was unremarkable, apart from both girls showing signs of being distinctly weary and uncomfortable after two days in the saddle. When the town hove into sight Emily let out an excited squeal.

'Look, 'Mima, we're nearly home!' she cried.

It was early evening and they reined in on the slope above the town to finalize their plans. O'Shea had just drawn breath to set out his own views and opinions on what was to happen next when Jemima Covenay cut the ground from under his feet by announcing to her sister:

'Listen Emily, before we go home you're going to see Father Flaherty for a little while. You want to see his cats again, don't you?'

'Ooh yes. You think he'll let me give them a saucer of milk again, like I did before one time?'

'I'm sure of it. Me and Mr O'Shea have some business to tend to — just boring grown-up stuff. Is that all right?'

So enchanted was Emily at the thought that she might once more have the opportunity to offer milk to the priest's cats that she was quite oblivious to anything else.

''Course it is, 'Mima. Just as you say,' she said.

The older sister turned to O'Shea.

'Well that's settled, then,' she said.

'The devil it is!' he replied, but Jemima had already started down towards the town with her sister.

As they drew near to the church it seemed to Rick O'Shea considerably more than four or five days must have passed since he had gone into that place and been tricked into this mad adventure by that crafty old priest. But, totting it up in his head, he realized that less than a week had gone by since he'd made that strange confession.

The interior of the church was just as he remembered it and there, fussing about near the altar, was Father Flaherty himself. His face lit up in a smile of sheer joy when he caught sight of Emily Covenay, who skipped down the nave and threw her arms around the priest in a fierce hug.

'My sister said I can give your pussy cats a bowl of milk again, Father,' she said. 'Can I really?'

'To be sure you can, my child. I've been praying for you and now here you are.'

O'Shea spoke up. 'Would it be imposing upon you, Father, to leave the child in your care for a short time?' he asked. 'I have some business to attend to before she returns to her home.'

'Well, my son,' replied the priest, 'you came up trumps and no mistake. I knew you had it in you. I reckon as you've done all that I could have hoped. You and the church are square now. Of course Emily can stay here for as long as she wishes.'

He turned to Jemima. 'What in the name of all that's wonderful are you doing dressed up like that, child?' he asked. 'Sure and your poor father's almost out of his mind with worry. Are ye not ashamed of yourself?'

'Don't scold her, sir,' interrupted

O'Shea. 'Without this young lady's help we'd not have won our way safely back here.'

'Well now, you don't say so? So long as you don't fetch up here at mass on Sunday dressed in such a heathenish fashion, then I suppose it don't signify. What's this unfinished business you have, my boy?'

'I'd as soon not discuss it here, not in front of that little one,' said O'Shea. 'It's enough that those as did that dreadful thing might be moving towards a reckoning.'

Father Flaherty toyed with the idea of reminding this grim-looking young fellow of that scriptural text that touches upon vengeance being the proper business of the Lord and not for men to take into their own hands. Then he looked at the innocent face of Emily Covenay and said instead:

'Sure, it says in the Good Book that anybody who offends against one of these little ones, it were better for that man that he had a millstone tied round his neck and was flung into the ocean. You go and do what you have to do, but be sure to come back here again in one piece. You'll be wanting a blessing before you set sail across the sea back to dear old Ireland again, I'll be bound.'

'Thank you, Father.'

Rick O'Shea turned and strode from the church, this being meant as a hint to Jemima Covenay that her presence was neither needed nor wanted. Unfortunately, she was impervious to such slights and quickly caught him up, so that by the time he had left the church behind she was walking alongside him.

'Well,' she said, 'what do we do now?'

O'Shea stopped dead in the little square in front of the church.

'There's no 'we' in the case,' he said. 'I shall be acting alone. You've had your little bit of adventure, now be getting yourself off home to your pa.'

This sharp speech failed to have the desired effect, for the young woman merely snorted derisively.

'I mind that I saved your bacon

already and may do so again,' she said. 'This is my affair every bit as much as it's yours. More, for it's my family as that man has interfered with.'

They had left the three horses on a hitching post down the way and O'Shea toyed with the idea of just running off, mounting up and trying to lose Jemima in that way. He had, though, an uncomfortable feeling that this might not work and that she would be likely to catch up with him.

'This is a damned nuisance,' he said irritably. 'Can I say nothing to persuade you to leave this to me?'

'If that Yanez has a heap o' men with him, then you might not be able to take them all by your own self. Why won't you own that it makes more sense this way?'

'We can't stand here talking of murder and mayhem on the public highway,' said O'Shea. 'I hope to sell this feeble nag that I picked up in Archangel. Come along with me and we'll talk more.'

Despite himself, he was secretly pleased that Jemima was not going to leave him. He had grown accustomed to her presence over the last few days and there was also something in what she said. Her skill with a rifle might very well make the difference between life and death for him. All the same, he felt guilty at the thought that she had already done murder once in his company, back on the ferry to Archangel. It would be a terrible thing to encourage such a young woman to kill another man.

To O'Shea's immense surprise and enormous gratification, he managed to dispose of the horse that he had acquired at only a little less than he had paid for it. He and Jemima retired to a little place that sold fruit juice and soda pop along with various sweetmeats. As they sat there, sipping cold drinks, he said in a low voice, so that none of the other patrons would overhear:

'Yanez feels he has cause to seek my death. Maybe he's right. I never harmed a woman before in my life and I'm sorry that his mother came to such an end. I know these Spanish Catholics, they worship their mothers. Make them out to be like the Mother Mary herself. He won't rest 'til he's settled with me.'

'What will you do?'

'Offer him a duel, I guess. It's the least I can do. I can't just walk away, for he might even yet try to kill your sister to silence her mouth. For good or ill, I must finish what I began.'

There was little more to be said and so the two of them sat in companionable silence for a few minutes. Then Jemima spoke again.

'If what you say is true, then I must take word to my pa. With Sheriff Jackson gone, we've got no law hereabouts, so I reckon that we'll all need to take care of our own business for a spell. If you really don't need my help, I'll ride out now. Father Flaherty will keep Emily safe and out of the way. I'll speak to him of it before going.'

So it was that the two of them parted

amicably, although for his part O'Shea still felt an urge to apologize to the young woman for getting her into a position where she had been obliged to shoot a man. He had, despite his rough life, a very conventional view of what was right and proper for men and women and firing rifles at bandits fell most definitely into that sphere of action more properly inhabited by men. *Mind,* he thought admiringly, *it's lucky enough for me that she was willing and able to press that trigger. It would have been all up with me, else!*

A visit to the Girl of the Period seemed to be called for. Surely he might hear of any useful gossip there, was the reasoning that took Rick O'Shea in that direction, rather than any desire for intoxicating liquor. No sooner had he entered than a man he knew slightly came up to him.

'Word is that you're wanted for murder,' was whispered in his ear.

'Murder?' he echoed in amazement, wondering how news of Seth Jackson's violent death could possibly have reached town ahead of him. 'Who's after me, then?'

'It's said as you were out on the scout with Jack Flynn. Robbing a train. There's three men as was deputized lying dead in this here town and feelings are running high.'

'Ah shit! I'd forgot about that.'

The other man gave O'Shea a strange look, as though he could scarcely believe that a man might be mixed up in three murders and then forget all about them.

'I tipped you the wink, as you would me,' was all he said. Then he walked off, leaving Rick O'Shea to wonder whether he ought to ask any questions now or simply leave town and make for New York, as had been his plan before this present business blew up. Then he turned on his heel and left the saloon, almost bumping into Valentin Yanez, who was on his way in.

The two men paused in their tracks for the merest fraction of a second, before they both came to the same conclusion. A gun battle here on Main Street in a civilized town like this would have but one ending. Whoever died, the survivor would without doubt be seized and held until some enquiries had been made. They might be able to slip out of the coils for such a death, pleading self-defence or some such, but both of them knew that they were wanted on capital charges and that, whoever won the duel, the winner would still end up dangling from a rope.

Powerful as Yanez's thirst for vengeance was, he had no intention of casting away his own life in the quest for O'Shea's death. He could accomplish that without risking his neck. For his own part, Rick O'Shea knew that if any trouble in which he played a part erupted now, there was every chance that some man who had been in that posse up at the Gap would take him and that could easily end in a lynching.

San Angelo was a civilized town but, after the deaths of three deputies, it was altogether possible that the citizens would not want any shilly-shallying in dealing with the man they thought answerable. A trial might be a luxury that they were disinclined to grant him.

All these thoughts went through Yanez's and O'Shea's minds in next to no time and the result was that they did not even make eye contact, but simply carried on walking, passing each other. Without looking back, O'Shea strode along to where he'd left the mare and swung himself into the saddle. Then he trotted north towards where he supposed the Covenay spread to be.

With young Emily safely in the keeping of the priest, he could forget about her. But still he had some responsibility for his actions in rescuing the child. He had, however unwittingly, caused the death of Yanez's mother and brought the bandit across the Rio Grande in pursuit. After all that the poor father of the two girls had suffered over the last week or two, the stealing away of one child and the vanishing of another, it would be a scurvy trick to play on the man to lead a band of such desperadoes to his door and then to dig up and leave him to deal with it. No, what he had begun, he must finish.

O'Shea figured that the best thing he could do would be to ride along towards Tom Covenay's place and see whether anything suggested itself to him on the way. He'd an idea that Yanez would fetch up there sooner or later, to silence the child who could tell so much about him and his men. Yanez wasn't to know that she was simple-minded; he would most likely see her as a dangerous witness to be rendered harmless as soon as possible.

There was great suspicion against Yanez and his men in Southern Texas, it being widely supposed that he was behind many robberies and murders, but here was a witness who could pin a capital charge on him. He would certainly make a move to put the girl out of the way. Then again, if Jemima had not yet returned home, he, O'Shea, might be able to put a father's mind at ease and let him know that both girls were safe. It would be a wonder if the poor man hadn't been driven out of his senses by worry.

An hour's trot along the track leading north from San Angelo brought O'Shea to a collection of fields at the centre of which was a large, stone-built house, surrounded by various stables, barns and other wooden structures. It certainly looked a pretty prosperous operation. But then there were many men like Tom Covenay — especially since the agricultural recession — with plenty of land under the plough, but without more than a few dollars in cash money at their disposal.

A black maid answered the door and looked doubtfully at O'Shea, as though unsure whether he was a beggar or tradesman who should be directed round to the rear of the house. He couldn't blame her; he looked pretty damned rough after the last few days' adventures.

'Is your master in?' he asked. 'Meaning Tom Covenay. This is his house?'

'Master's lying abed. He don't want t'see nobody.'

'He'll want to see me. Has his daughter returned yet?'

The woman looked at him suspiciously.

'Miss Em'ly and Miss J'mima, they ain't neither of 'em here,' she said.

'I've news of them. Please tell your master and see if he won't receive me. I'll wait here.'

The maid went off and Rick O'Shea reflected on why it so often seemed to be the way that when you tried to do the right thing, it often turned out a sight harder and more complicated than simply doing wrong in the first place. Everything about the events since that wretched confession of his tended to confirm him in this view. After two minutes or so, the maid returned.

'Master'll see you upstairs,' she said.

Once he was inside the house O'Shea

could see immediately that, although evidently once luxurious, the place was now looking a little faded and past its prime. There was evidence of mending and patching and a generally run-down air. Having led him upstairs, the maid knocked on a door and announced:

'Gent'man t'see you, suh.'

She turned the handle of the door and, without entering, merely indicated that O'Shea was to go in. He did so, whereupon the door was closed noiselessly behind him. He found himself facing an elderly, white-haired man who was sitting up in bed. The most noticeable feature of this old man was that he had a pistol levelled at O'Shea; pointing, in fact, straight at his chest.

9

The old man in the bed said nothing for a second or two and then remarked in a conversational tone of voice:

'I knew one of you bastards would turn up here when I couldn't pay your ransom. You may have my daughter, but by God, one of you at least'll die for it.'

'You think I'm one of them as took your daughter, sir? Not a bit of it.'

The man in the bed looked at O'Shea in amazement.

'You're never a Donegal man?' he said. 'What's afoot? You best answer me quickly now.'

Without glossing over anything, O'Shea told Tom Covenay the whole story, not even bothering to conceal the fact that he'd been set the task of rescuing Emily as a penance. Once he'd been assured that his daughters were safe, the old man listened with evident enjoyment to the whole story. At the end of it he said:

'So Father Flaherty set a thief to catch a thief, did he? The sly old fox. And you're the poacher turned gamekeeper yourself, is that the way of it? Well I'm damned!'

With an agility that surprised O'Shea, since this was a man who had recently been lying abed like an invalid, old Tom Covenay leaped from his bed. 'I'd best dress,' he said. 'Turn your back, young man. I ain't minded as you should see me naked.'

When he'd turned round, O'Shea said: 'I understood you were prostrate, Mr Covenay.'

'I was despairing of my life, boy, not ailing physically. You have children of your own?'

'I ain't had that pleasure, no.'

'Then you wouldn't understand. I was ready to die. You say my Jemima acquitted herself well?'

'I wouldn't have made it back alive without her. It would have been all up with your younger daughter too if Miss Jemima hadn't taken a hand in the matter.'

'She handled the rifle well enough too, you say? I taught her to shoot, you know.'

'So she gave me to understand,' said O'Shea. 'Yes, she's a dead shot with the thing. I never saw the like.'

'That's my girl! You think these rascals are likely to show up here, Mr O'Shea?'

'I can't see where else they'd go, sir. Their leader is set on having my blood and he knows I'm somewhere in the area.'

'Well, my boy, I tell you now, I won't rest until I've killed every one of those sons of the Devil. You're with me, I dare say?'

'Well, it's my affair now too, so I don't see that I have a choice.'

For a man who had until a matter of minutes earlier been confined to his bed, Tom Covenay appeared to be possessed of extraordinary reserves of energy and vigour. He had dressed himself in rough working clothes, like he was off to ride the range. For a man of his age — he couldn't have been a day under sixty-five — the effect was striking and a little disconcerting. The old man caught the look on O'Shea's face.

'What's wrong with you, boy?' he said sharply. 'You never see a man dressed for work? You only got that pistol? You'll need a rifle, I shouldn't wonder.'

'I have one out in my pack, thank you.'

'I got better than that,' said Tom Covenay with perfect assurance, without even asking what weapon O'Shea had. 'Come down now and we'll find something for you.'

As the two men made their way down the stairs, old Mr Covenay leading the way, he turned and said over his shoulder:

'You think Jemima is due back at any moment?'

'So I understood. Last I saw of her, she was going to caution Father Flaherty to keep your younger daughter out of sight until this was cleared up. Then she was coming back here.'

Mr Covenay stopped dead in his tracks, almost causing O'Shea to bump into him.

'And that rapscallion, this Yanez,' he said, 'he knows for certain-sure that you're in and around the neighbourhood now. You've no doubt of that?'

'None whatever.'

'Why then, the sooner we kill him and his men the better.'

Rick O'Shea was very far from being of a delicate or sensitive nature, but the casual way that the old man had announced his intention of killing a bunch of men sent goose-bumps all over him. Something of what he was feeling must have shown in his face, because Tom Covenay said:

'While they had my little Emily I couldn't do a damned thing for fear of her being harmed. That's what drove me to despair. Then when her sister went as well, I thought I would have died. But now? I'll give it to those boys hot and strong, see if I don't.'

In the kitchen was a walk-in closet, which was stacked with weaponry.

'I call this my armoury,' the old man said. 'We had a lot of trouble here when first I settled, and my men had to fight. Seemed silly to get rid of the guns when it was all over, so here they are. Help yourself, boy.'

At thirty years of age Rick O'Shea found it more than a little irksome to be addressed in this way as 'boy', but he figured that it would do him no harm. The maid who had answered the door to him was pottering round in the kitchen. She had said, as they entered the kitchen: 'Sure is good to see you out o' bed, suh.' As the two men emerged from the closet, both with rifles that they proceeded to load, the woman left the stove and went to the window.

'Got more company,' she remarked.

Those were fated to be the last words

she ever spoke in this world. The window shattered and there came the crack of musketry from outside the house. The ball took the black maid in the throat and as they watched, she fell to the ground shaking and convulsing, great gouts of blood spurting from the mortal wound that she had received.

Both men threw themselves to the floor. It was clear that there was nothing to be done for the dying woman and they had more pressing concerns than saying a prayer for the repose of her soul. O'Shea risked a quick look from the window and almost paid for it with his life. There was a furious outbreak of firing, which sent a veritable storm of broken glass flying into the two men sheltering on the floor.

'There's three of them that I can see,' said O'Shea. 'Most likely more round the front. They don't know I'm here and aim to take the house and wait for me and Emily to return, so's they can kill us both.'

'No doubt,' said Tom Covenay, and O'Shea marvelled at the old man's phlegmatic acceptance of the trap in which they found themselves. 'What d'ye propose?'

'I'm going to scoot upstairs and work from there. Can you fire a few times through this window? Don't bother aiming or putting yourself in danger, just give them something to think about. I've an idea that they still don't expect resistance. Probably think there's only domestics and an invalid in the place.'

'They'll learn different,' said the old man grimly. 'Go on, off with ye.'

Crawling through the broken and splintered glass was painful; O'Shea found that his hands were bloody by the time that he had gained the hallway. This put him in just the frame of mind to inflict pain on others and, as he strode up the stairs, he cocked the rifle in readiness. The first and most urgent need was to deal with those who would soon be pressing close to the rear of the house, where old Mr Covenay was currently sheltering.

By good fortune the window in the bedroom at the rear of the house was already open: perhaps the room was being aired. Whatever the reason, the open window fitted O'Shea's purposes perfectly. He wasted no time in thinking things over, but simply crossed the room to the window, took aim at the three men below and snapped off two shots. He had the immense satisfaction of seeing one of the men fall from his horse and the other crying out in pain and wheeling his mount round.

He ducked back out of sight immediately as a ball came whistling through the open window and buried itself in the ceiling, sending down a shower of powdered plaster. From below came the sound of two shots fired from inside the house. Figuring that Tom Covenay would keep the pot boiling nicely on that side of the house, O'Shea sprinted across the landing towards the rooms overlooking the front entrance. He was just in time.

There were three more men at the front of the house, including Yanez, who was mounted on a fine black stallion. His two confederates had dismounted and were making their way to the front door with the evident intention of forcing an entry. Both men died without even knowing that they were in peril.

Perhaps they had thought that seizing the house and waiting for their prey to fetch up there would be an easy job: just a question of murdering a maid and killing an old man lying in his bed. With two quick, well-aimed shots, O'Shea drilled bloody holes in the top of both of the dismounted riders' heads. He turned to deal in the same way with Yanez, but the Mexican had spurred his horse and galloped round the side of the house to see what was doing there.

There was no time to lose; O'Shea could hear shots coming from the area of the kitchen. He ran back to the bedroom that overlooked the back of the house, hoping to repeat his trick of catching men unawares and disposing of them without their even knowing what had hit them, but the surviving attackers were now alert to the danger they were in and were hiding behind a stone wall running along to the barn.

From what O'Shea could make out at a quick glance there were only two of them, with Yanez presumably hiding at the side of the house out of sight from the windows. One of the men must have caught a glimpse of O'Shea, who had to leap back as a ball passed so close to his head that he heard its passing, as though an angry hornet had just buzzed near his ear. Things were certainly hotting up.

Peering round the edge of the window cautiously, O'Shea risked another shot. He had to withdraw swiftly; splinters of wood flew into his cheek as a ball clipped the window frame. It was a classic stand-off and the battle could easily go on for an hour if both sides were careful and nobody took any foolish or unnecessary risks. Of course, such a confrontation ultimately favoured the coolheaded and dispassionate and, in general, vicious bandits tended more towards the impulsive and aggressive. There was also the little matter of the advantage that defenders always enjoyed in such matches. All that O'Shea and old Mr Covenay needed to do was stay put. It was those who hoped to invade and occupy the house who would, sooner or later, be forced to break from cover.

So it proved, because as O'Shea peeped around the window he saw one of the men behind the wall jump to his feet and begin jinking towards the kitchen door. As O'Shea was about to draw down on the fellow, the remaining man, firing from the cover of the wall, let loose with three or four rapid shots, so that O'Shea was unable to take careful aim himself.

From down below there came a spintering crash, which O'Shea guessed was the kitchen door being kicked in; it was followed by two shots that sounded almost simultaneous. At pretty much the same moment the other man got to his feet, left the cover of the wall and began heading for the house. Unfortunately for him he had nobody to cover him; O'Shea shot him down like a dog before he had covered more than a half-dozen paces. Then he raced down the stairs, wondering as he did so what he might find.

The first thing to be seen on entering the kitchen was the body of one of the bandits sprawled across the threshold, a stream of blood snaking across the paved floor from a wound in the man's chest. He was plainly dead, so O'Shea turned his attention to Tom Covenay, who was drenched in blood and looking none too good.

'God almighty!' cried O'Shea. 'Where are you hit?'

'Never mind that,' replied the old man irritably. 'Have we settled 'em all?'

'No, the leader's out there somewhere.'

'Well, go and kill him, you fool! What are you hanging about here for?'

'You'll be all right?'

Tom Covenay made an impatient gesture, so O'Shea, his piece cocked, darted from the house, scanning anxiously with his eyes from left to right, hoping to spot Yanez before the Mexican saw him.

There was no sign of Yanez; the only thing that O'Shea could think was that the man had ridden off when he saw that all his boys had been taken out. He didn't, perhaps, fancy his chances of mounting a lone assault on the defended position.

When O'Shea returned to the kitchen old Mr Covenay was still in the same position.

'Where are you hit?' O'Shea asked.

'Shoulder. It's not hit the bone. Sliced through a vein, though.'

'You want I should put on a tourniquet?'

'And make me lose my arm? Don't think it for a moment. You know how a little blood can make much of itself. I'll do well enough. No sign of the leader of those bastards?'

'He must have dug up when he saw that all his boys had been killed. He's finished, you needn't fret about him. He'll be lucky to make it back across the Rio Grande. Let's get you more comfortable.'

'Don't fuss. You're like a woman. I'm fine.'

It was apparent that Tom Covenay was anything but fine, however, for as soon as he got to his feet he proceeded to faint from loss of blood, crashing to the flagstones like a felled oak. Somehow O'Shea managed to get the man propped up against the wall. When he had done so he ripped up a towel and used this as a makeshift field dressing. It would slow down and eventually stop the bleeding. Just as the old man had said, this was a flesh wound, which would bleed freely but not so much that the victim would be put in hazard of his life. A little bloodletting would do the choleric old fellow no harm at all.

Mindful of the fact that Jemima Covenay would most likely be back before too long, O'Shea set himself to making the kitchen look a little less like an abattoir; it was awash with gore and stank of shed blood. The first step was to dispose of the corpse of the man who had kicked down the door and, so O'Shea supposed, had shot Tom Covenay.

He dragged the man out by his heels with as little ceremony as he might have shifted the carcass of a butchered hog. O'Shea had, in the usual way of things, a feeling of respect for those slain violently in this way, but he was exceedingly ill-disposed towards these men, so he simply dumped the body out of sight behind the wall. Then he dragged the fellow's two *compadres* round so that they too were out of sight.

The black maid was a different matter: O'Shea had no intention of just shifting her out of the way like a sack of

210

potatoes. Supposing that she had probably been a servant for whom the family might have had some affection, O'Shea decided to lay her out in the front parlour. He had no idea if he was acting correctly, nevertheless he picked up the poor woman and then laid her gently on the long table in the parlour. Whatever the Covenays might or might not have wanted, he wasn't about to leave a woman's corpse lying on the floor like that.

Having dealt with the bodies in the house, O'Shea found a bucket and mop and sluiced down the flags to remove every trace of blood. When he had finished the kitchen looked a little more decent. Old Mr Covenay had come to by this time.

'Where's Hannah?' he asked.

'Your maid? I laid her out in the parlour. Hope I weren't overstepping the mark?'

'No, you did the right thing, Mr O'Shea. She's been with us many years, poor woman. Thank you.'

'I ain't fussing, but I reckon as I ought to get you into bed, sir. You need to rest up.'

'You're in the right, of course. I feel as weak as a kitten. No sign yet of Jemima?'

'No, but I aim to ride back to San Angelo and see what's become of her. Most like she's with that priest.'

Tom Covenay's eyes were shining as they talked of his elder daughter, of whom he was, it was plain, enormously proud.

'She really shot at those men when you crossed the river?'

'She really did, sir. I'm a dab hand with a pistol, but I tell you I couldn't shoot with a rifle the way that your daughter could. She saved all our lives.'

'Yes, that's my girl all right,' said the old man with great satisfaction. 'See if you can lend me a hand now in getting up those stairs, will you? I'm afeared I'll not be able to make it alone.'

It was somewhat of a struggle to make their way to the upper floor of the house, for being shot had taken more out of the elderly Tom Covenay than he was willing to admit. By the time they reached his bedroom he was whitefaced and panting.

'You . . . need a hand . . . getting your clothes off?' asked O'Shea tentatively.

'No,' replied Covenay ungraciously. 'The day I can't get my own pants off I might as well be in my grave.'

Rick O'Shea shrugged. From all that he was able to collect he had now done as much for the Covenay family as could reasonably be expected.

Although he had left an item or two of luggage in his room at San Angelo, he didn't think that it would be a smart move to go back and fetch it. Just his luck if he ended up being hanged for three murders he'd had no part in. No, he would ride along the railroad line and take the train a few miles north of here. Once he was out of Pecos County, he'd be home and dry. *New York, here I come!*

After establishing that there was nothing at all that he could do for the old man, who wanted only to be left in peace, Rick O'Shea bade him farewell and prepared to shake the dust of that place from his feet, as scripture has it. There were still two corpses to deal with, those of the two men he'd shot in front of the house, so before leaving he hauled them round the side of the house and dumped them with the other men. Then, partly from force of habit, and also because he cared about dumb animals, he untacked the dead men's horses and turned them out to graze in the field behind the barn. All in all, he thought, as he looked round, he'd tidied up well enough. Nobody would guess that there had been a bloody skirmish here not a half-hour since; one which had left five men dead.

Back in the house O'Shea took a final look in the kitchen and assured himself that there was nothing to alarm Jemima Covenay when she returned. He had the feeling anyway that it would take more than a corpse or two to put that young lady out of countenance. Then he thought he'd set off towards San Angelo and just see if he might meet her on the road. He didn't plan to enter the town itself, though.

At the last moment he realized that he was carrying Tom Covenay's rifle and knew that he had best leave it behind. He worked the handle and ejected the remaining cartridges, which he placed neatly on the kitchen table. Then he leaned the weapon itself against the wall and walked out of the kitchen door.

He found himself face to face with Valentin Yanez, who had a rifle held at his hip, pointing at O'Shea.

'I thought you'd be running for the border by now, Yanez,' observed O'Shea amiably. 'Never thought you'd hang round here, not with all your men being dead and all.'

'You have cost me everything,' said the bandit. 'Everything. Even my own mother and brother.' His voice rose to a scream. 'My own mother! Dead!'

Although he was perfectly aware that his life was now balanced on the edge of the sharpest knife you ever saw, Rick O'Shea could not forbear to mention his views on this.

'The old lady had a little girl tied to her like a dog, Yanez,' he said. 'You play tricks like that, it's apt to end badly. Ain't there something in the Good Book about those who live by the sword dying by the same means?'

It was a wonderful thing to O'Shea that he was able to talk so calmly, now that all his hopes were dashed and he was sure that he would never set eyes on Ireland again after all.

'As for your men,' he continued, 'well, they knew the game when they started. I don't see as I'm answerable for them. It was kill or be killed.'

'You will see that my weapon is cocked and I will tell you that I've taken first pull on the trigger,' Yanez told him. 'Take out that pistol with your left hand and throw it away. Only pull it with two fingers; don't grasp the hilt.'

O'Shea noted, having tossed away his only hope for living, as though it were happening to somebody else, that even when a man knows that he is to die he will do whatever it takes to live even a few seconds longer. There could be not the faintest doubt that the Mexican was going to kill him and it would make sense now for O'Shea to launch a sudden desperate assault against the man who was pointing the rifle at him.

Even so, he just stood there, hoping to live just a little longer. He felt vaguely disgusted with himself. But then he thought: *if a man is to die, isn't it better that he should face it calmly instead of struggling and fighting?*

'What became of your friend in the house?' asked Yanez. 'Does he live still?'

'Yes, he's resting in his bed. Took a ball to his shoulder.'

'Good. After you are dead I shall kill him and then burn down his house.'

'While we're talking plain, Yanez, I might as well tell you that you needn't rely on Sheriff Jackson any more in the future. He met with an accident.'

'Jackson is dead?'

'As the proverbial doornail.'

Yanez absorbed this information, not taking his eyes from O'Shea, nor giving any sign at all that he was not giving the other man his undivided attention. He looked to be brooding and O'Shea wondered if a little bluffing might be in order.

'Tell you what, Yanez,' he said, 'you're pretty much washed up here. You ride off now, I won't say a thing to anybody. I've no interest in seeing you caught. Go off and we'll be done with each other.'

O'Shea's words appeared to rouse Yanez from his thoughts.

'I'm going to kill you very slowly, my meddling friend,' he said. 'First, I shall shoot your ankles, then I shall kick you around a little. Then I'm going to fire at your knees, and after that your worthless balls. Then we'll see how long I let you live before I finish you off.'

'You talk a lot, Yanez. Let's be done with it.'

'You are afraid, I think?'

'That's my affair.'

The Mexican raised his rifle and took aim at O'Shea's legs. It was impossible that O'Shea would be able to jump the man; maybe it would be more manly just to take what was coming without giving the appearance of fear or flinching away like a wounded cur. Better to meet death in this way, like a man.

Yanez sensed that something had changed in the other man's demeanour and for a moment he looked puzzled, even a little uncertain. O'Shea looked back steadily and fearlessly, and was immensely surprised when Yanez's head jerked suddenly to one side, as though he had been punched. Instinctively, O'Shea stepped back, so that if the rifle went off, it wouldn't hit him. But there was no present prospect of that happening, because Yanez plummeted to the ground, where he lay quite still.

From all that O'Shea could make out the man was stone dead.

10

O'Shea had been so pent up with the nervous effort of bracing himself to meet a painful and humiliating death that he hadn't heard the shot that had saved his life. He glanced up at the window at the back of the house, with the vague notion that Tom Covenay had recovered sufficiently to wield a weapon, but there was no sign of anything like that. He went over to the body and took the rifle from Yanez's lifeless grasp. It would do no harm to be prepared when there was shooting coming from an unknown source.

Then everything fell into place as Jemima Covenay stood up from the long grass of a little hillock which lay some quarter-mile from the house. She raised a hand in salute, then vanished from sight again. A short while later she rode round the side of the little hill on her horse, which had apparently been kept out of sight on the opposite slope. The young woman was seemingly in no hurry, for she just let the horse make its own pace, which was a leisurely walk. When she came closer she hailed O'Shea.

'I guess that's thrice now I've saved your life, Mr O'Shea.'

'I reckon that's a fact, Miss Jemima,' he called back. 'I couldn't argue with that. You took that devil with a head shot at . . . what, a quarter-mile? That's the hell of a piece of shooting, if you'll forgive my language.'

When she had come even closer and no longer had to shout, Jemima Covenay spoke again.

'This is a pretty remarkable rifle, you know. My pa told me that at some shooting match in England, before the war, they fixed up one of these Whitworths in a vice and their Queen Victoria fired it by pulling a piece of string tied round the trigger. Scored a bull at four hundred yards.'

All this talk of guns and shooting didn't somehow seem fitting to O'Shea in a young lady. He had been feeling increasingly guilty about putting Jemima Covenay into situations where she had to shoot men. He tried to put some of this into words as she dismounted, but she laughed off his apologies.

'I told you,' she said, 'I wanted to kill every last one of those men as took my little sister. When I saw this 'un drawing down on you, I could tell at once he was one of them and that he was about to shoot you into the bargain. I ain't a bit sorry to have shot him.'

'Well, this is him that was behind the whole scheme, so you've finished off the thing altogether now.'

'Where's my father? Is he all right?'

'He is and he isn't.'

'What's that supposed to mean?'

'Fact is,' explained O'Shea awkwardly, 'we had a bit of a set-to here and he stopped a ball in his shoulder.'

'He's alive?'

'Yes, of course. I helped him to bed.'

'Hannah's safe and sound? I don't see her around.'

Although she was a remarkably tough girl, when O'Shea broke the news of the maid's death, Jemima Covenay started weeping like a child, which embarrassed O'Shea to no small extent. She had cheerfully committed murder and even fired with deadly intent at the county sheriff, but the loss of this servant was too much for her. The sight of women crying had always been one of those things that left Rick O'Shea at a loss to know what to do.

Now he stood there uselessly, muttering things such as: 'There, there,' and 'Don't take on so.'

After a while she stopped and glared fiercely at O'Shea.

'You needn't think I'm a baby, neither. It's just that I have known Hannah since I was a little girl. We're right fond of her.'

'Is your sister safe with the good father?' O'Shea asked, to change the subject.

'She's having the time of her life. Father Flaherty makes a regular pet of her and lets her do just as she pleases. He's that fond of Emily.'

'He seems a good man for all that he got me embroiled in this pickle. Shall we go and see how your father's doing?'

'To be sure. Mother of God! What's that behind the wall there?'

'Some of the men who came here, hoping to kill your family — and me, of course. I'm afraid there's two more at the front of the house.'

'Well,' said Jemima practically, 'I guess we'll have to deal with them later.'

Mr Covenay was sleeping peacefully when they entered his bedroom; so peacefully in fact, that his daughter panicked and shook him roughly, for fear that he was dead. When he saw who it was, the old man became irascible. 'Sure, and where d'ye think you have been gadding off to, missy, with me out of my mind with worry?'

'I had to see about our Emily, Pa. She's safe and sound now.'

'By heaven! I should be fetching my riding crop to you, child, for giving me such a scare. And what's become of your hair?'

'It's a long story. This here is Mr O'Shea — '

'Yes,' said Tom Covenay, 'I've met the gentleman and ended up being shot for me trouble. Well, at any rate I hear you've acquitted yourself well enough with that gun o' mine. I suppose it's all worked out well enough in the end.'

Despite Covenay's scolding tone it was very plain to O'Shea that the old man was so proud of his daughter that he had to put on a show of being angry to conceal the fact. His daughter did not look as though she were at all deceived by all this and smiled broadly at her father.

'Come then, you young scapegrace,' he said in a milder tone, 'and give your pa a hug.'

It was very nearly nightfall and

O'Shea gratefully accepted the offer of a bed for the night before setting off for New York the following day. He sketched briefly the misunderstanding that had rendered it impossible for him to return to San Angelo, and neither Tom Covenay nor his daughter asked for any further details. They both figured that whatever Rick O'Shea might have done in the past, they had no business enquiring about it after all that he had undertaken on behalf of their family.

They ate up in the old man's bedroom: an impromptu, picnic meal which had a pleasing informality and intimacy about it. During the meal O'Shea mentioned something that had been on his mind and might work to the advantage of his hosts.

'I'll be off early tomorrow,' he said, 'so you'll forgive me if I say this bluntly now. I'm gathering that you're not overly blessed with money right at this moment?'

'Who's been saying such a thing?'

asked Tom Covenay angrily. 'I'll be damned if I'll have my business voiced abroad! Where'd you hear that?'

'Father Flaherty told me,' replied O'Shea apologetically. 'I'm not just gossiping. I've a reason for asking about this.'

'Go on, Mr O'Shea,' said Jemima. 'What are you driving at?'

'Here's the way of it. There's a five-thousand-dollar reward offered by some newpaper for the safe return of your sister, and I don't know if they'd consent to pay a family member on that offer. But there's six bandits scattered outside this house and I'm certain-sure that there'll be rewards payable on some of them. On Yanez, certainly, without a shadow of a doubt. You could get somebody over from San Angelo and try to claim on them. Might bring you in a little cash.'

Both Covenays digested this information in silence. After a space, Mr Covenay spoke.

'You might have a point there, boy.

You might just. Worth trying, when all's said and done.'

* * *

The following morning, Rick O'Shea took his leave of the Covenays: father and daughter. The old man was as curmudgeonly as ever, remarking that he heartily disliked long, protracted farewells and that if O'Shea were going, then he'd best be on the road without any further ado.

Tom Covenay had been bullied by his daughter into remaining in his bed for the day, the wound in his shoulder having opened up in the night and drenched the bedclothes in blood. Before O'Shea left, he shook hands with Mr Covenay, who gripped his hand with crushing force and said huskily:

'Never did one man owe more to another than I do to you, young man. May God bless and keep you.'

Now it was O'Shea's turn to make

light of the obligation.

'Ah, we Irishers must stick together in this heathen land,' he replied.

Downstairs he found that Jemima had prepared a meal for him to eat on the journey.

'I'll never forget what you did for us, you know,' she said. 'Sorry if I wasn't the most pleasant company on the road.'

'They say fine words butter no parsnips. You saved my life more than once; I reckon that amounts to more than a few fancy airs and graces.'

'You wouldn't think of staying here for a few days, I suppose?' she asked wistfully.

'What, and run the risk of having my neck stretched when some of those boys in San Angelo find I'm here and invite me to a necktie party? You'll have to get somebody here today to identify those bodies and see about any reward money, you know. They'll be stinking the place out before long.'

'I guess you're right. Well then, we'd best part now.'

Suddenly, and without either of them planning it, the two young people found themselves embracing; not in a passionate clinch, but more as brother and sister bidding each other farewell. Then O'Shea picked up his gear and went out to tack up the mare. Jemima Covenay gazed after him for a moment or two, then went upstairs to see if there was anything she could do for her father.

Epilogue

After spending years in the arid landscapes of Texas, Arizona and New Mexico, the thing that most struck Rick O'Shea as he rode along the lane towards the property which his brother had acquired for them was how lush and green everything was. Not for nothing did they call this the 'Emerald Isle'. The other sensation that he had — and he was sure this would pass in time — was just how small and poky everything seemed here; compared, that was, with what he had been used to. Instead of the wide, open plains and endless vistas where there often wasn't another living soul to be seen, all that was visible, in this part of Donegal at any rate, were narrow lanes, and fields the size of pocket handkerchiefs. O'Shea supposed that he would in time get used to it; this was where he had been born and raised when all was said and done.

O'Shea's brother was not a whale for writing and ciphering and the directions that he had sent for finding the farm, which he had purchased with the money that Rick O'Shea had sent him, were not altogether as clear as could be wished. Nevertheless, after asking for directions from a number of loafers and itinerants, O'Shea thought he was now on the right track.

Then the lane he was riding along widened out and there it was; a white farmhouse surrounded by neat fields, such as an English Protestant might have envied. Glory! His endeavours had not been in vain.

As he rode up the gravel drive the front door opened and there was his mammy, who had doubtless been sitting and looking out of the window all morning, awaiting her eldest son's arrival. As soon as he leaped from his horse, his mother enfolded him in her arms and began weeping with joy. This didn't last long, though, for she was not a woman given to unbridled emotion and always felt a little ashamed after any display of that sort. She stepped back a pace from her son.

'Sure and you've not been eating well lately and that's a fact,' she said. 'I can see it by the look of ye.'

'I'm fine, Mammy.'

'And when did you last make your confession, son? Don't be lying to me now.'

'I made my confession not a fortnight before taking ship for the old country.'

'Ah, Richard, sure and I raised ye right. It's a proud woman I'll be when we all go to mass this Sunday.'

Mother and son turned and went into the house. Rick O'Shea knew that from then onwards he would for evermore be 'Richard' or even just plain 'Dick'. There'd be no more 'Rick O'Shea' in this life for him.